Amy Cross is the author of more than 250 horror, paranormal, fantasy and thriller novels.

OTHER TITLES
BY AMY CROSS INCLUDE

THE HAUNTING OF OXENDON SCHOOL

THE GHOSTS OF ROSE RADCLIFFE BOOK 4

AMY CROSS

CONTENTS

THE
HAUNTING
OF
OXENDON
SCHOOL

CHAPTER ONE

"OKAY, ROSE. I WANT you to concentrate really hard. I want you to look at the back of the card I'm holding and try again to imagine what's on the other side. Remember, it could be any number from one to ten, or it could be a jack, a queen or a king. And it could be a heart, a diamond, a club or a spade. The only thing it *can't* be is a joker. I don't want you to rush, I want you to really take your time and think carefully. Now... what card am I holding?"

Sitting on a kitchen chair next to the fridge, with several wires running from a bunch of sensors attached to her body, Rose stared at the card and tried to be helpful.

She furrowed her brow.

She stared at the card until she felt as if her

eyes might be about to fall out.

She remembered to breathe slowly.

She did all the things that Jonathan had told her – repeatedly – were so important.

And finally, even though she hadn't really come up with anything, she decided to try for a guess.

"The... four," she said cautiously.

"Of?"

"Of..."

She furrowed her brow a little more, and after a moment she actually began to feel slightly confident in her selection, as if she might genuinely be able to sense something.

"Hearts," she said, still watching the card. "The four of hearts."

Jonathan made a note, and then he set the nine of clubs back down into the bottom of the deck.

"Did I get it right?" Rose asked.

"Let's just focus on the test," he replied diplomatically, glancing at the long list of crosses on the page and the few ticks. "It's not about getting it right or wrong, Rose, it's about seeing what you can and can't do. Do you remember what I told you at the end of last year when we started this project? There are no wrong answers, there's only data and information. I just want to see whether we can recreate any of the things that happened to you while I was at Lotham Lodge. You want to understand those things a little better too, don't you?"

She thought for a few seconds, and then she nodded. In truth, she didn't want to think about her seizures at all, but she knew the investigation was important to Jonathan and part of her worried that – if she was no longer useful – the Pearsons might decide to send her away.

Not Rebecca, perhaps.

Rebecca seemed to genuinely like her.

But sometimes she wondered about Jonathan. Everything about him just felt so cold and clinical.

"So on we go," he continued, holding up another card, this time the king of diamonds. "Don't worry, Rose, I know you're probably getting tired. We'll just do another hundred and then we'll call it a day."

"A hundred?" she replied, clearly dispirited by that notion.

And yet...

And yet she knew she had to try.

"Okay."

"Right," he said, before taking a deep

breath. "I want you to concentrate extra hard on this particular card. I want you to look at the back of it and really try to imagine what's on the other side. Try to picture what I'm seeing in your head. Remember, it might be a heart, a diamond, a club or a spade. I don't want you to rush, I want you to take your time and think carefully. The only thing it can't be is a joker. Now, Rose... can you tell me what card I'm holding?"

***

"She had a success rate of 1.72%," Jonathan muttered under his breath as he stood in the front room and looked through the notes once more. "That's very slightly below average. There's nothing in the data here, or in the readings from the sensors, to show anything unusual happening at all. She just seems so..."

He turned to the next page.

"Normal," he mused, not even bothering to hide his disappointment.

He turned to yet another page.

"I'm calling it," he added. "This approach isn't working. Whatever happened last year to allow Rose to somehow... connect with what was going on at Lotham Lodge, I'm not going to be able to recreate it through a bunch of stupid card games. And I saw it in her eyes, too. She's just as lost as I am. The kid doesn't have a clue."

A moment later, realizing that he hadn't heard a reply for several minutes, he turned and saw that his wife was still reading something on her laptop.

"Honey?"

"What?" she replied, glancing over at him with the expression of someone who'd very much not heard a word he was saying. "Oh, I'm sorry, I was looking at this stair rail system for Mum. It's cheaper than the other ones but it seems to be just as good, and it's not a full lift, so she might be more willing to consider it."

"Or she could move into a bungalow."

"Do you seriously think my mother would ever willingly lose even a shred of her independence?" Rebecca asked. "I've tried a million times to get her to think about moving out of that little cottage, but she won't consider going anywhere else. I get it, she lived there with Dad so she's attached to it on a sentimental level, but she's had two falls now in six months and I'm worried she might really hurt herself next time. And this rail thing would just about fit into that twisty little staircase. I wish she could see that she needs to rethink things."

"That cottage was built for hobbits," he replied. "I know people were generally a little shorter back in the day, but that place is ridiculous. I have to go down those stairs backwards."

"I'm going to have to go down and see her again."

"I'm busy that week."

"I didn't say when I'm going."

"I'm still busy," he told her. "Joking aside, I'm almost drowning in paperwork. Even if I wanted to join you, I just can't, at least not for the next month or two. I'm -"

"You're busy, I know," she replied before he could finish, as she closed the laptop and set it aside. "But I've put this off for long enough. I need to go and see her and try to get her used to the idea of... a little change. I know she's as stubborn as anything, but she has to see reason eventually. If she wants to still go off on jaunts a couple of times a year with her friends from the W.I., she needs to keep herself in good shape. That means not falling over all the time."

"You should phrase it like that," he suggested. "Exactly like that. Use those words."

"There's just the question of the girls," she added.

He sighed.

"I *can* take them," she told him. "Mum's got two spare bedrooms, so they could squeeze into one together. But I was just thinking, this might be a good chance for you to... spend a little more time with them."

"I'm extremely busy."

"We're both extremely busy."

"Yes, but my work is -"

He caught himself just in time.

"More important?" she asked, raising one eyebrow.

"You know what I mean," he continued. "The plan has always been for me to get this project done so that I can spend more time on our little side investigations. It's a balancing act, Rebecca, and -"

"I know," she said, getting to her feet, "and it's fine. Honestly. I'll take them down to Oxendon with me for a long weekend."

"And I'll use that time to really get stuck in. By Monday, I might actually be finished."

"Don't offer miracles you can't deliver," she replied. "Just... promise me that you're genuinely too busy. I hate to think that you're still finding it difficult to spend time around Rose."

She waited, but now he was focusing on the notebooks.

"Jonathan? Do you remember Rose? The little girl we took in a while back? The one you don't seem to have much of a rapport with yet?"

"I admit that I never quite know how to talk to her, but we've been doing well with the tests. She follows my instructions carefully and tries her best."

"Yes, but she's a ten-year-old girl," she countered, "not a lab rat."

"You're the one who suggested that we ought to conduct the tests alone," he reminded her. "You said it might be a way for us to bond."

"And look how that's going," she said under her breath, even though she knew there was no point arguing. "Listen, it's fine, you know I don't mind taking them on a road trip." Stepping closer, she kissed him on the cheek. "They're getting along pretty well now but a change of scenery might do them good."

"So you're *not* worried about Rose settling in now? You've changed your tune."

"I'm more worried about you," she told him. "You keep coming up with these tests to run on her, and it must be bugging you that none of them ever seem to work. Sooner or later we might have to start thinking of some other way to classify whatever... abilities Rose might or might not have."

"There's something about her," he pointed

out. "She hasn't had a single seizure since last year and the doctors still can't explain what happened back then. There are too many coincidences to ignore and I *know* she had some kind of awareness of what was happening to me at Lotham Lodge. Sometimes I even think that without her, I might have..."

His voice trailed off.

"You know what I mean," he added, preferring to avoid getting into too much detail about his worst fears. "There's definitely something going on in that girl's head. I might not have found the right test just yet, but sooner or later... I'm going to figure out why she seems so different."

CHAPTER TWO

ONE DAY LATER, AS she pushed the car door open, Rose stepped out onto the gravel road and looked all around. For a moment, stretching a little after two hours spent in the cramped rear of the car, she could only take in the calm, quiet atmosphere of the village.

"It sucks here," Alicia said, stepping out after her and then pushing the door shut. "There's nothing to do. It's the most boring place in the whole world."

"It smells weird," Rose pointed out, turning to look past the church and out toward the distant rolling fields. "It smells almost like..."

"Poo," Alicia continued. "This whole place stinks."

"That's the farmers working on the fields," Rebecca said as she opened the boot. "You might not like it, but without them, we wouldn't have very much to eat."

"But do they have to make *everything* smell so bad?" Alicia asked, turning to her mother.

"It's the smell of nature," Rebecca suggested. "Of the real world. Of... life itself. And the world is never neat and tidy. I actually like it out here, it's good to get away from the towns and cities once in a while. You should think of this weekend break as a chance to reconnect with the soil."

"Why would I want to reconnect with soil?" Alicia asked. "Soil's dirty."

"How old is that church?" Rose asked, looking at the lightly-colored stone church beyond a nearby low wall.

"I'm not exactly sure," Rebecca said as she closed the boot again, "but I think it's several hundred years old, at least. I've been in there a few times when Jonathan and I visited for Christmas, it's really beautiful. And a few times when I was closer to your age. If it's open, you girls should take a look."

As soon as she heard that suggestion, Alicia scrunched her nose up.

"How many people live here?" Rose asked,

looking at a nearby row of cottages.

"Not many," Rebecca told her. "Two hundred, maybe?"

"Only two hundred?" Rose replied, clearly shocked by that number. "What do they do? There can't be many jobs here. Where do they shop? Do they even *have* a shop here? They must have a pub, everywhere has a pub. Do they have a school? What about a library?"

"You're really full of questions, huh?" Rebecca replied, unable to stifle a faint smile. "Well, a lot of the people here are retired, but there are businesses around that employ the rest. There are a couple of shops, actually, and there's a nice little pub that does the best Sunday roasts you'll ever have in your life. There used to be a village school but I think it shut a while ago, now the children go to one in the next village along. And as for a library, there's a mobile one that comes through about once a week. Anything else you'd like to know?"

Rose thought for a moment, before shaking her head.

"Not now," she told Rebecca, "but I'll let you know if something else comes up."

"I'm sure you will," Rebecca said, clearly amused as she began to carry her bag over to one of the cottages. "Come on, Nana Evelyn probably has lunch ready for us. You haven't even met her yet, Rose. You're in for a surprise."

"Is she scary?" Rose asked, turning to Alicia. "Is your grandmother scary?"

"She's special," Alicia replied, with a hint of foreboding in her voice. "That's what Dad always says about her, anyway. She's just really... really... *really* special."

"That sounds good," Rose said, before hesitating for a moment. "Special's good, isn't it? It must be good to be special." She hesitated again as she began to realize that Alicia didn't seem at all enthusiastic. "What's wrong with being special?"

"Oh, you'll see," Alicia said with a smile. "You're about to find out. And your belly isn't going to like it very much."

***

"And this," Evelyn said as she set another plate on the table, "is my new sow thistle and acorn custard, with just a hint of the samphire that I picked last week when I was down in Dorset. And the dark green paste is something that I made myself with the extra burdock and nettles I had at the bottom of the garden."

"Nettles?" Rose replied, staring in wide-eyed astonishment at the assorted items on various plates. "Like... stinging nettles?"

"Yes, but they won't sting you now," Evelyn explained. "Go on, don't be scared. I'd never serve up anything that wasn't completely safe and utterly delicious."

Rose thought for a moment, before reaching over and picking up a piece of rock-hard bread, which she used to scoop up some of the custard.

"That's the spirit," Evelyn said with a grin. "Rebecca, your new guest has a very adventurous spirit. I like seeing that in someone so young."

Hearing a slurping sound, she turned to see that Alicia was noisily sucking on a straw that she'd inserted into a can of soda.

"Others," the elderly woman continued, with evident disapproval, "might want to learn to more fully embrace the wonders of the world around us. Where is that awful concoction from, anyway? I can smell it from here, it's absolutely foul."

"Alicia likes her pop," Rebecca reminded her mother. "Don't worry, we brought some food that she likes. Not everyone want to eat things that have been foraged from hedgerows, Mum."

"Ultra-processed rubbish," Evelyn said,

shaking her head as she turned and limped back to the counter. "It's not good for anyone in the long run, you know. Our stomachs are home to billions of microscopic organisms that need to be nurtured and looked after. If we're not in harmony with them, and communing with their needs, we're on a slippery slope to disaster."

"Is that what you're doing with your home-brewed beer?" Rebecca asked. "You're communing with microscopic organisms?"

"Darling, it's ale," Evelyn countered, "and by making it myself, I can ensure that it's completely natural and that it doesn't contain anything nasty whatsoever. The organisms get very offended if we try to feed them processed rubbish. They know when their needs are being ignored and they have a tendency to rebel. There's nothing better for your tummy than -"

Before she could finish, she let out a loud clap of wind from her backside.

"There's no way around it," she continued as she began to sort through various jars. "Excuse me. But there's no way way around it, one should positively worship all the organisms in our bellies. Without them, we'd all be dead inside of an hour. Life is a balance. It's no wonder there's so much sickness in the world when people consume industrially-produced commercial garbage."

"Told you she's special," Alicia whispered, nudging Rose's arm. "She could fart for England."

"This is really weird," Rose replied, having tasted a mouthful of the custard. "My tongue feels fuzzy."

"You're probably getting high."

"She's not getting high!" Rebecca hissed, before grabbing the pot and giving it a sniff. "Mum, there's nothing untoward in any of this, is there?"

"Heavens, no!" Evelyn protested. "I wouldn't give anything like that to a child. I know how prim and proper you are, Rebecca. I couldn't be doing with all the lectures I'd receive."

She turned and winked at the girls.

"I'm not prim and proper," Rebecca sighed. "I just... like to stay in the middle lane, that's all."

"You weren't like that until you met Jonathan," Evelyn told her. "You were such a free-spirited little girl, I raised you to embrace the wonders of the natural world. Then you met him and he tamed you, he seduced you with the shallow comforts of modernity and now look at you, living in such a built-up area and probably inhaling all sorts of fumes every day. You're probably even being poisoned while you sleep. Did you know that micro-plastics can even be found in bed linen these days?"

Rebecca opened her mouth to argue, before remembering at the last second that there was really no point.

"My tongue's ticklish," Rose said, chewing very slowly on another piece of bread. "I think my teeth are going numb. Or my gums. I can't quite tell."

"We'll have proper food later," Alicia whispered. "Mum's got bags of it in our room."

"Mum, how's your leg after the fall?" Rebecca asked, watching as her mother limped over to the fridge. "I came down here to see how you're doing and to discuss the possibility of installing something to stop it happening again."

"I don't need gadgets in my home," Evelyn replied dismissively. "You know what I think about that sort of thing. Why should I compromise my -"

Suddenly she let out a brief burp.

"Pardon me," she continued as she took a glass jar from the fridge and held it up to examine the fizzy pale green liquid inside, "but why should I compromise my home when I don't need such things? All that electrical energy seeps into the air and I'm sure it's disturbing my pickle jars."

"It'd stop me having to rush down here every time you hurt yourself," Rebecca pointed out, sounding a little more irritated now. "Have you thought about that? The saving in petrol alone would be immense. Couldn't you get something installed just to make *my* life easier?"

"Mum, can we go outside while you argue with Nana Evelyn?" Alicia asked.

"We're not arguing," Rebecca said firmly. "We're just... discussing the possibilities."

"Yes, but you'll start arguing soon, you always do," Alicia pointed out. "Please, can Rose and I go and play somewhere outside? I promise we won't go far."

CHAPTER THREE

BY THE TIME THEY reached the other side of the road opposite the cottage, both Rose and Alicia could already hear raised voices coming from inside. Stopping, they turned and looked at the window just as Rebecca could be heard yelling.

"This *always* happens when we arrive," Alicia explained wearily. "Nana Evelyn's the only person who knows how to wind Mum up so badly, and Mum can't help it. Don't worry, they'll be tired soon and there won't be another argument for the rest of our visit. It's so predictable, it's like clockwork."

"I feel like my nose is on fire," Rose replied.

"That'll be something Nana Evelyn gave you," Alicia said, turning to her with a smile. "She spends all her time foraging for things in the countryside. Her food's really... odd. One time, after dinner here, Mum pretended to take me out for a walk, but actually she drove me and her to a burger place in the next village and we had these really nice juicy burgers. If we're lucky, she might do the same thing tonight, but if she does, we're not allowed to tell Nana Evelyn, although I think she knows anyway."

"What are they arguing *about*?" Rose asked as she watched the cottage and heard the raised voices still shouting at each other.

"This time it's some stair thing that Mum wants Nana Evelyn to get," Alicia told her, "but really it's just the usual stuff about how Mum thinks she should be more responsible and Nana Evelyn thinks Mum worries too much. They love each other really, but Nana Evelyn drives Mum up the wall sometimes. I suppose all families are like that in some ways. I wish Nana Evelyn wouldn't fart so much, but she says it's a sign of a healthy belly. I still don't like it, though."

Turning, she saw that Rose had wandered over to a set of stone steps that led up into the churchyard.

"Rose? Do you want to explore?" she asked, heading over to join her. "There's not much up there except gravestones, but they're pretty cool. Some of them are ancient, they're from four or five hundred years ago. Sometimes it freaks me out to think of all the skeletons buried in there, just rotting away in coffins underground." She paused before turning to Rose and studying the side of her face for a moment. "You're not too chicken to go in and see, are you?"

"I'm not scared of ghosts," Rose whispered.

"Good, then let's take a look," Alicia said, skipping up the steps and slipping through the gate. "Come on, Rose, don't lag behind! Last one into the cemetery has to try Nana Evelyn's weird ice cream later! And trust me, you do *not* want to do that. If you think your tongue feels weird now, wait until after dinner! Snails should never be in ice cream!"

***

"Abraham... something," Alicia said as she leaned closer to the cracked old gravestone and tried to decipher the words, "and his wife... Catherine... something?"

Reaching out, she tried to scratch some moss away from the mottled surface.

"Careful," Rose said, "it's wobbling."

"A lot of them do that," Alicia replied,

before turning to look back at some of the other stones. After a moment she pointed at one in particular, which had a piece of wood propping it up. "That one'd probably topple all the way over if you took the wood away. Think about it, someone buried that person four hundred years ago and ever since the stone has just stood there, slowly starting to lean a little more each year."

She paused for a moment as a gentle breeze blew through the cemetery.

"I like places like this," she added. "They're really calm and peaceful. I just wish you couldn't always smell the poo the farmers spread on their fields. Sometimes that smell makes me want to be sick. I don't like to see my food until it's in the supermarket, because then it's clean."

Making her way past some more stones, Rose seemed lost in thought. She reached out and touched the tops of the stones, letting her hands linger for longer on some than others, until finally she stopped in front of one particular grave and stared down at the stone cylinder that ran along its length.

"Those ones are weird," Alicia admitted. "It's as if people in the old days used to have a competition to see who could come up with the weirdest design for their grave. There's one over there that's like a little mausoleum, and it's got a metal railing all around it to stop people climbing onto the top, but I don't think that really stops many people at all. Not if they're determined."

She waited for a reply, but after a moment she realized that Rose was still staring at the cylindrical grave while keeping one hand lighting resting on the stone.

"What are you doing?" she added.

Again she waited, and again Rose seemed utterly lost in thought. Realizing that something seemed to be bothering her, Alicia began to make her way over, but even her approach across the tall grass failed to stir Rose or bring out any kind of reaction. Finally, reaching out, Alicia touched the same stone and waited, but all she felt was the rough surface with its display of green and blue and yellow moss.

"What?" she asked. "Rose, are you okay? You haven't said anything for a while."

"It's just sad," Rose whispered, staring intently at the stone now, not even blinking. "When you think about it, I mean. It's really sad that all those bodies are left down in the ground."

"What are you talking about?"

"They're just reminders of lives that were lived a long time ago," Rose said quietly.

"Sometimes you can feel an echo of how they felt when they died, but that's all it is most of the time."

"It's... just a cemetery," Alicia replied after a suitable pause. "Yeah, it's sad, but people die."

"I know that," Rose said, turning to her suddenly. "I just think it's sad to think about, that's all."

She hesitated, and after a moment Alicia realized that her attention appeared to have been caught by something further off in the distance. Turning to follow Rose's gaze, at first she saw only more gravestones and a couple of trees, before finally she spotted a fairly small and low building beyond the cemetery's far end. And then, before she had a chance to wonder out loud what the building might be, Rose brushed against her shoulder and began to make her way across the grass.

"Where are you going?" Alicia called after her. "I don't think we should be out for too long. Mum and Nana Evelyn have probably stopped arguing by now!"

She waited, but Rose was now walking directly toward the distant building.

"Fine," Alicia muttered under her breath, setting off after her.

By the time she caught up, Rose had stopped in front of the building and appeared to be lost in something of a daze.

"It looks old," Alicia pointed out, staring at the dusty windows and feeling a sliver of fear run through her body. "It almost looks like it's been abandoned. There are lots of weeds in front of the door."

Spotting a sign nearby, she walked over and pulled some branches away.

"Oxendon School," she read out loud. "Mum said there used to be one, but it looks like it closed years ago."

Letting the branches fall back into place, she turned to see that Rose was slowly stepping toward the front of the building.

"It's pretty spooky," Alicia continued. "Don't you think? I bet no-one has been in there for years and years. It's not very big, though, so there can't have been many children. Then again, Oxendon's not a very big village so they probably didn't need very big classes. Maybe there was only one teacher."

Looking at the back of Rose's head, she was used by now to the fact that she rarely received a reply. Making her way over, she had to step around some old wooden posts that appeared to have once been part of a fence. As she reached Rose again, she looked once more at the dirty windows and wondered what the place might be like inside, although she had no real desire to find out.

"I bet it's cold," she said softly. "It must be, if it's been left like this for so long. Don't you think so?"

"It's haunted," Rose replied.

Alicia turned to her.

"There's a ghost in there," Rose continued, and now her voice sounded almost flat, as if she was mesmerized by the sight of the place. Reaching out, she touched the wall. "She's all alone."

"How... how do you know that?" Alicia asked.

"How can you *not*?" Rose replied, still touching the building. "Can't you feel its presence?"

"I can just feel that it's cold out here," Alicia said, struggling slightly to keep from getting freaked out. Looking at the school again, she had to admit that it was pretty spooky – but at the same time she saw no hint of a ghost. "Did you see something moving in one of the windows?"

Rose shook her head.

"Then what makes you think that there's a ghost in there?"

"I just know," Rose said firmly. "I can't explain it. I just do."

"Girls?" Rebecca called out in the distance.

"Alicia? Rose? Where are you?"

"We should get back," Alicia pointed out. "Rose, I know Dad's been running lots of tests on you, but you mustn't let him make you believe weird things. If you didn't even see someone at a window or... or hear someone, then there's no way you could think that there's a ghost in there. You're probably just scared because it looks so weird."

"Alicia?" Rebecca shouted. "Rose, where are you?"

"Come on," Alicia said, grabbing Rose by the hand and leading her back across the cemetery. "We can't stay out here all day. We should get back to Nana's house so she can freak us out with more weirdness."

CHAPTER FOUR

"AND WE THANK YOU for this meal, as we thank you for all our meals. Amen."

"Amen," Rebecca said softly, and the girls did the same.

"Alright," Evelyn said with a glint of excitement in her eyes, "tuck in."

Sitting around the cramped dining room table, Rebecca and the girls weren't really sure where to begin. Having been busy in the kitchen for a couple of hours, and having conspicuously refused to say exactly what she was cooking, Evelyn had finally emerged with a plate containing an entire roasted rabbit – complete with the head and even the ears still attached.

"I caught it myself," she said proudly.

"Of course you did," Rebecca replied.

"It's actually a very nutritious meal," Evelyn continued. "I know you city dwellers are used to your processed meat, but rabbit has long been a staple part of the diet round these parts. You know, back in the day, a feast like this would have been reserved for the king or perhaps a few of his most highly favored courtiers. Lowly peasants such as ourselves would be lucky to dine on something so magnificent so much as once a year."

She looked over at Alicia.

"Granted," she added, "most people remove the head before cooking, but I like to follow a very old and very traditional recipe from the days when absolutely nothing went to waste. Would either of you girls like the honor of eating one of the ears?"

Alicia and Rose stared at the rabbit for a moment in silence, before both slowly shaking their heads.

"All the more for me, then," Evelyn said, reaching over and carefully slicing away one of the ears. "I shall leave the other one just in case you become more adventurous."

"Your grandma used to make rabbit for me when I was your age," Rebecca told the girls. "It's actually not that unusual." She leaned closer to Alicia. "Believe me, there are a *lot* of worse things she could have dished up."

"I heard that," Evelyn said sharply. "As it happens, I had originally intended to serve a lovely badger stew, but I just couldn't acquire the meat in time. Obviously one has to be a little careful to avoid breaking any laws regarding badgers, but I know a few farmers round these parts who tend to quite miraculously end up with a surprising number of dead specimens, and they're only too happy to let me help dispose of the evidence."

"That sounds pretty illegal, Mum," Rebecca pointed out.

"It's only illegal if one agrees with the law that's being broken."

"That's not how it works," Rebecca said, before turning to the girls again. "Ignore everything you just heard. You absolutely can't ignore laws that you don't agree with."

"You're making them both so... conventional," Evelyn continued. "If you keep on like this, how will you ever get them to experience the joy of breaking the rules? Not everyone wants to grow up and conform to all the so-called laws of society, you know."

"Let me cut you a nice piece," Rebecca said, clearly taking great care to avoid getting into another argument as she took the carving knife and began to remove some meat from one side of the rabbit. "Alicia, can you pass me your plate first? I know this might seem a little strange, but trust me, it's actually very nice and tasty. Just try not to look at the head too much, or that one remaining ear. Or the eyeballs. My mother has always had a talent for culinary theatricality."

***

A couple of hours later, standing on the landing, Rose peered at a set of twigs and grass that appeared to have been twisted and formed into something approximating a human shape. The result had been hung from a nail on the wall.

Rebecca was downstairs on the phone, talking to Jonathan, while Alicia could be heard brushing her teeth in the bathroom. Rose, meanwhile, had loitered on the landing after her own ablutions and was now rather struck by the many strange decorations in Evelyn's cottage. There were lots of small framed pictures showing old-fashioned people engaged in a variety of strange acts, often involving animals that were apparently dancing, and a few of the images even depicted people who'd been tied to wooden posts as flames burned near their feet. In fact, the more she looked at these pictures, the more Rose felt as if she was peeking into some long-lost hidden world.

The twig and grass human figure was hanging between two of the pictures, and even from a distance of a foot or so away, Rose could just about detect a slightly musty smell.

Behind her a floorboard creaked, and she

turned just in time to see Evelyn emerging from one of the other bedrooms wearing a faded old white nightgown.

"There you are," the old woman said with a friendly smile. Her white hair, freed from various clips, was now enormous and frizzy. "Waiting for bedtime, are you?"

Rose nodded.

"I hope you don't find any of those pictures too scary," Evelyn continued, limping over to join her. "I inherited them from my father – Rebecca's grandfather – and he, I believe, inherited them from his own parents. They're old images from the area around Oxendon, showing various traditional rituals and customs that used to be pursued by the people who lived here. I'm sure they seem quite strange to a young lady such as yourself, but down here in this part of Kent we have a rich history of folklore. Well, it's the same in every part of the country, but I always feel as if Kent and Sussex and the southern counties all the way along to Cornwall have customs that contain just a little extra twist of..."

She paused as she tried to think of the right word.

"Darkness," she added finally with a smile. "And jet black humor. You don't have to go too far to find blood in the countryside around here."

"What do you mean?" Rose asked.

"Never you mind."

"Is that woman being hurt?" Rose continued, pointing at the drawing of a woman on top of a fire. "It looks like they're burning her."

"Would it surprise you to know that women were often accused of witchcraft round these parts? f" Evelyn asked. "That sort of thing isn't as far back in the past as some people would like us all to believe. Even I might well have faced such accusations had I lived a couple of centuries earlier."

"You?" Rose thought for a moment. "Why?"

"You've seen all the unusual delicacies I cook up," Evelyn reminded her. "To some, those are beautiful and cheap meals, but to others they might seem like witchcraft. Don't worry, I never add eye of newt to any of my recipes and I certainly don't possess any special powers, but I like to think that in some small way I'm carrying on a few of our shared ancient traditions. Rebecca finds me embarrassing, I know that, but when she was your age she didn't feel quite the same way."

"She didn't?"

"I used to take her out on foraging trips," Evelyn explained with a slightly sad, melancholic tone to her voice. "We'd spend hours searching the hedgerows, looking for plants or mushrooms I could use. I was always very careful, I never let her touch a mushroom I wasn't sure of. And I always thought she enjoyed those trips so much. She certainly seemed to. And then, as she got older and became more interested in her sciences and her career, something changed. She started making fun of me. I try to hide it, but to be honest with you, it hurts every time she belittles my cooking or acts like I'm just some foolish old woman."

"I think she's worried about you living here by yourself," Rose suggested.

"I know that, but she doesn't need to fret. I'm old enough and ugly enough to look after myself. I just wish she'd remember the fun we used to have, that's all. I wish she'd stop treating me like some mad old kook."

Hearing the bathroom door unlocking, she leaned closer.

"I shouldn't have said some of those things," she whispered. "Please don't spread them to Alicia or Rebecca."

"Do you need the bathroom?" Alicia asked cautiously as she emerged onto the landing.

"No," Rose said, shaking her head, "I was just looking at all these pictures."

"Some of them are really creepy," Alicia suggested. "Sorry, Nana, but it's true. Why have you got pictures of people being burned at the stake?"

"Just a friendly reminder of the past," Evelyn told her with a sad smile. "You must never allow yourself to forget the past, either of you. It's just as important as the present and the future.

Sometimes things you think are long gone – quite awful things – suddenly come back. But I think Rebecca's finished on the phone, she'll be up soon so I'd better bugger off to bed." She patted Rose on the shoulder as she walked away. "Sleep well, girls. I don't know what we're going to do tomorrow, but I'm sure it'll be a lot of fun."

"What were you talking to her about?" Alicia whispered once Evelyn had disappeared into the nearby bedroom and had pushed the door shut.

"Nothing much," Rose said, looking up once again at the crude human figure hanging between some of the paintings. "I like her, though. She's really interesting. And even though I don't understand a lot of what she was talking about, I like hearing her talk." She stared at the figure for a moment longer. "I'm really tired now," she added finally. "I think I need to go to sleep."

CHAPTER FIVE

AN OWL HOOTED SOMEWHERE in the distance as Alicia opened her eyes. Having drifted off to sleep in the cottage's small third bedroom, she was now suddenly wide awake.

Turning to her left, she looked at the window and saw the church on the other side of the street. Moonlight was picking out the tops of all the gravestones, and for a few seconds she couldn't help but feel that the sight was strangely spooky. And then, just as she was about to roll back over and try to go to sleep, she realized that she could see a figure walking slowly between the stones, heading further and further away across the cemetery just as the moonlight faded and the scene was plunged into darkness.

Looking over at the other bed, she saw to

her horror that the sheets had been pulled aside and that there was no sign of Rose.

"No!" she whispered, clambering out of bed. "Why are you doing this? Why do you always have to be weird?"

***

"Rose?" she called out a couple of minutes later, trying to be both loud and subtle as she hurried through the cemetery. "Where are you? Rose, this is so stupid! You have to go back to bed!"

Almost tripping on the bumpy ground, she steadied herself against one of the cold gravestones as she picked her way around to the far side of the church and looked around for any sign of Rose's whereabouts. Having very carefully crept out of the cottage without making so much as a sound, she was now clinging to the hope that she might somehow manage to drag Rose back before anyone knew that the pair of them had even got out of bed. With each second that passed, however, that plan was feeling more and more threadbare.

"Where are you?" she whispered under her breath. "Come on, Rose, it's cold out here. Why can't you just stay in bed like a normal person?"

Reaching the far end of the cemetery, she stopped and looked around, yet there was still no sign of Rose anywhere. Feeling increasingly desperate, and starting to worry that perhaps she should have woken her mother after all, she realized that by now Rose could be anywhere. She turned to hurry back to the cottage and raise the alarm, but at the last second she froze as she glanced at the old school building and saw that something was different.

The front door, which during the day had been shut, was now hanging wide open.

"Rose?" she said cautiously, before starting to make her way over. "You'd better not be in there, Rose. I swear, if you are, I'm going to be so mad!"

Slowing her pace as she approached the door, she realized that she absolutely positively didn't want to set foot inside the school. Stopping, she looked inside and saw only darkness, although after a moment her eyes adjusted a little and she began to make out a corridor stretching deeper into the building with doors leading off on either side to what she could only assume must be classrooms.

A moment later, at the far end of that corridor, a figure briefly moved in the darkness before disappearing from view – as if it had slipped into one of the rooms on the left.

"Rose?" Alicia shouted, stepping even closer to the doorway but stopping at the last second. "Rose, stop being stupid! You have to come back to the cottage!"

Looking down, she saw that her foot was

almost – but not quite – over the threshold. As she looked along the corridor, she began to wonder whether the dark figure could have been Rose at all, since it had seemed almost a little too tall. At the same time, she reminded herself that she needed to stay calm, and a moment later she heard the distinct sound of footsteps moving loudly across the floor of one of the rooms, as if hard shoes were banging against the wooden boards.

"Rose, it's late and I'm cold," she whined, hoping against hope that her words might finally break through. "I know you probably think this is fun, but for me it's really annoying. And if Mum finds out there we're here, she's going to go ballistic. You've never seen her when she's really angry, but trust me, it's really not very nice."

She listened as the footsteps receded, seemingly heading further away into one of the building's half dozen or so rooms. Finally the place fell silent again, and although she wondered just how Rose could have made such a loud noise while walking, Alicia really didn't give the matter too much thought; instead she lingered for a moment longer in the doorway before sighing as she realized that she really had no choice.

Stepping into the corridor, she immediately felt a floorboard bend slightly beneath her left foot, along with a very subtle creaking sound.

"Rose, what are you doing here?" she asked,

daring to raise her voice a little more now even as she felt that the air inside the school was much colder. "This place is really creepy."

Reaching out, she flicked an old switch on the wall, but no lights flickered to life.

"I didn't have to follow you out here, you know," she continued, stepping forward. "I could have just gone back to sleep and let Mum find out in the morning that you went out. Or I could have woken her up and told her that you were gone, and then she would have really freaked out. You'd be in so much trouble."

Walking past an open doorway, she looked through and saw a room with just some hooks on the walls.

"You should be so grateful to me," she said, looking into another room and seeing empty shelves that she assumed must have once been filled with books. "Most people wouldn't come out here like this. They'd just stay tucked up in bed, and they'd let you get into whatever trouble you want."

Looking into another room, she saw some kind of kitchen, and then – as she reached the next door – she peered through and stopped as soon as she spotted several rows of old wooden desks with chairs neatly arranged behind them. And at the far end of the room, sitting up straight and staring toward the front, Rose appeared to have not even noticed now that she had company.

"What are you doing in here?" Alicia asked, hurrying past the desks and making her way over. "You're not even wearing a coat. You must be freezing."

Looking down, she was surprised to see Rose's bare feet. She glanced around for a pair of shoes, since she knew that bare feet couldn't have made such a loud noise earlier, and then she turned to look at the girl again.

"Rose, you're being weird," she complained. "Seriously, we're supposed to be asleep right now. I like going on adventures, just like you do, but if we're really tired in the morning Mum's going to know that something's up. But if you come back right now, I promise I won't tell her anything. Is that a deal?"

As she waited for an answer, she could already tell that Rose was once again lost in some kind of daze. Turning, she looked across the darkened room. There was just enough moonlight breaking through the grimy windows to illuminate the rows of desks and another larger desk at the front, with a blackboard on the wall at the end. The room was mostly bare, which Alicia figured was because it hadn't been used in a while, but something about all the empty chairs made her feel more than a little uncomfortable.

Looking at the nearest chair, she thought of all the people who must have sat there over the years, and who no doubt now were much older – or long gone.

Suddenly she heard a brief click, and she instantly turned and looked at the larger chair behind the larger desk at the head of the room.

"It was probably just a mouse or something," she said under her breath, even as she struggled to shake the feeling that in some way she was being watched.

As dust drifted through the moonlight, she looked around again before finally turning to Rose.

"Where are your shoes?" she asked. "Come on, I'm being serious, if you don't come back with me right now then I'll... I'll leave you here. Do you understand? I'll leave you right here and I'll go back to Nana's house and I won't even care if you get into trouble. I'll tell Mum that I tried to make you do the right thing but that you refused and -"

"She's here," Rose said, cutting her off.

"What? Who is?"

Alicia hesitated.

"Do you mean Mum?"

Slowly Rose shook her head.

"Do you mean Nana?"

Rose was still shaking her head, while staring at the teacher's desk.

"Then who *do* you mean?" Alicia asked, unable to hide her sense of frustration now. "Rose, you're being really annoying. There's no -"

Before she could finish, she heard the footsteps again, marching briskly through another room but this time edging closer and closer. Turning, she looked toward the open doorway as she realized that somebody was about to enter from the corridor.

"I told you, this place is haunted," Rose said softly, barely daring to raise her voice above a whisper. "There's a ghost here and... and she's noticed us."

CHAPTER SIX

FOR A MOMENT, AS she continued to stare at Rose, Alicia really wasn't sure what to think.

She'd heard her parents discussing the supernatural – when they thought she wasn't listening, of course – so she was certainly open to the possibility, and she knew that something pretty crazy had happened to her father at Lotham Lodge. She was also very much accustomed to the idea that Rose seemed to have a certain insight into such things, even if she got the sense that her father's experiments with the sensors and the monitors and the playing cards hadn't really led to much.

With all that acknowledged, however, she wasn't completely sure that she believed in ghosts herself. Some part of her simply couldn't quite wrap itself around the possibility that dead people might actually return to the world of the living; she didn't believe that the dead – who were supposed to be gone – could actually walk in the land of the living... at least, not until a fraction of a second later, when she heard the footsteps entering the room and she realized that somebody was standing behind her.

"She's here," Rose said, looking up slightly as her eyes opened wider than ever.

"Who... who is?" Alicia asked, not daring to turn around just yet.

"She's right here," Rose stammered.

"Who is?" Alicia snapped angrily.

She waited, but Rose was still staring.

Realizing that she wasn't going to get any easy answers, Alicia hesitated for a few more seconds before telling herself that she really needed to turn around. She still had to force herself to dredge up the courage, but finally – although she couldn't turn her whole body around – she at least managed to turn her head and look over her shoulder. At the same time, she opened her mouth ready to scream.

But she saw nobody.

Turning fully around, she felt a huge rush of relief as she saw that the rest of the classroom was still empty. She knew that the footsteps had been real, and that they'd seemed so very close, yet she figured that weird sounds could always be explained away; there was no actual sign of anyone, however, even though she could feel her heart pounding and she realized after a few more seconds that she was holding her breath.

Letting out a relieved sigh, she told herself that Rose had simply been trying to scare her – and that for a few seconds at least, she'd succeeded.

"She's alone," Rose said suddenly, whispering a little. "She's been alone for a long time. She walks from room to room, always searching for them, but she never finds them. She knows she's trapped here but she can't leave, not while there's still hope."

Slowly, Alicia turned to her.

"She doesn't know why we're here," Rose continued, still looking up as if she could see somebody towering above them both, "but she's not angry. She's just sad that we're not the ones she's looking for. She thinks that if she finds them, she can maybe be released, but until then... until then she can only keep looking, going from room to room endlessly, searching all day and all night, never even sleeping or -"

Gasping, she looked toward the door.

"She's going again," she added. "I think she lost interest in us. We don't matter to her. She doesn't want anything to disrupt her search."

"What are you talking about?" Alicia asked, feeling a little impatient now. "There wasn't anyone there. You're just making this up."

Rose continued to stare at the door.

"You're making it up!" Alicia said again, raising her voice a little.

"Don't shout," Rose whispered. "I don't think she'll like that."

"You're telling stupid stories," Alicia continued, "and I'm not going to believe them because -"

Suddenly a loud bang rang out, startling her so much that she hurried around to the other side of the desk so that she could stand side-by-side with Rose. Staring at the open doorway, she half expected to hear the footsteps again, but instead the old school building fell silent once more.

"I warned you," Rose said softly. "I don't know why, but she doesn't like people being loud."

"You're making this up," Alicia said, more cautiously this time. "I... I know you are."

"She thinks she needs silence to hear them," Rose continued. "It's like... she thinks if she listens hard enough, she'll be able to work out where they are. I don't know what that means, exactly, but she's calling to them and then she waits for them to reply." She turned to Alicia slowly. "I don't understand. Can't you hear her?"

"I can't hear anything," Alicia said firmly, "but I'm cold and I'm going back to Nana's cottage. Are you coming with me or do you want to stay here and waste time in an empty building?"

***

The grass crunched slightly beneath Alicia's feet as she hurried away from the old school. After a few more paces she stopped and looked back, and to her relief she saw that Rose was still following.

"Come on," she said firmly. "It's so cold out here."

As she got closer, Rose also stopped. She turned and looked back at the school, as if she was watching for some sign of movement.

"You're not going to go back inside, are you?" Alicia asked.

"It's so sad," Rose replied. "She's just trapped in there, going round and round, doing the same thing over and over and never finding whatever she's looking for."

"There was no-one there!"

"I don't know why I could hear her and you couldn't," Rose said cautiously. "It was so obvious to me, she was just right there in front of me and I could sort of... sense her fear and confusion."

"You're sounding really weird now," Alicia told her.

Hearing the sound of an engine, she looked across the cemetery just in time to see the lights of a car moving along the street. After a few seconds the engine sound stopped and the lights switched off.

"I can even feel it from here," Rose explained. "Some of it, at least. It's like there's so much sadness in that place and it's leaking out." She looked around for a moment at the moonlit grass. "Even if they don't understand why, people must sense that something's wrong here. They probably feel sad for no reason if they get close, so they probably stay away as much as they can. This whole area looks like it hasn't been disturbed very much. That must be why."

"Can we go back now?" Alicia asked as her teeth started to chatter. "It's really cold out here."

"It's a shame that no-one can help her," Rose said, finally setting off across the cemetery with Alicia hurrying alongside her. "I just don't know what anyone could do. I think she's been there for a very long time and -"

Stopping with no warning, she stared at some nearby gravestones before making her way over. Stopping at one of them, she reached out and touched the engraved words as if she was trying to read them using just her fingertips.

"This is hers," she added, looking down at the ground. "She's buried right here."

"I want to go!" Alicia insisted.

"I can't tell what her name was," Rose said, still feeling the moss-filled grooves on the stone's surface. "It's really hard to read. But I know it's her, and her body was buried here a long time ago but her ghost is still in the old school. She can't rest."

"Neither can I," Alicia replied, "because you won't let me. Come on, we're leaving!"

"It was a lonely funeral," Rose whispered. "I don't think anyone came. It was just the priest, and maybe the people who dug the hole. No-one else cared about her."

"We're going right now!"

Grabbing Rose's arm, Alicia forced her to follow and led her all the way to the stone steps. Making their way down, they quickly reached the road and hurried toward the cottage.

"We're going to have to sneak in really quietly," Alicia explained, "but don't worry, that shouldn't be too hard."

"Isn't the car in a different place?" Rose asked.

"What are you talking about?" Alicia said, still holding her arm as she glanced at the car outside the cottage. "I'm sure it must have -"

And then she stopped so suddenly that Rose actually bumped into her. Shocked, both girls stared into the car and saw Rebecca sitting in the driver's seat holding a fast food burger that she'd obviously taken from the brown paper bag on her lap. With her mouth open wide, Rebecca had clearly been about to take a bite before she'd been discovered and the expression in her eyes suggested that she knew full well that she'd been caught red-handed. Finally, reaching out, she wound the window down.

"What are you girls doing out here?" she stammered. "It's the middle of the night! You're supposed to be tucked up in bed!"

"Mum," Alicia said cautiously as her belly let out a faint rumble of hunger, "did you go to that twenty-four hour burger place again and not take us? That's so unfair! You know how much I love those burgers!"

CHAPTER SEVEN

"DANDELIONS MAKE FOR SUCH an underrated breakfast," Evelyn said the following morning as she filled a jug with water at the kitchen sink. "Much better than all those awful grain-based products that are always being shoved down the throats of the masses."

"Absolutely," Rebecca said, visibly grimacing a little as she slipped another of the strange patties into her mouth. "It's so great that you find all this stuff just growing around the village."

"Don't you buy *anything* from the shop?" Rose asked.

"A few necessities," Evelyn replied with a smile, "but no more than that. How can one hope to be connected to the natural world if one ignores the bounty it offers up to us every single day?"

She let out a brief burp.

"Pardon me," she added. "I must admit that one can get a little gassy on this sort of diet, but that's hardly unhealthy. And it's not as if we're at the opera or somewhere fancy. Who cares about some gas when you're with family?"

"Last night," Rose continued, "I -"

"I want to pop out after breakfast," Rebecca said, clearly making a determined effort to interrupt. She fixed Rose with a glare that was designed to remind her of their agreement. "Mum, you don't mind looking after the girls for a few hours, do you? I just want to... look around for old time's sake."

"I'll be only too happy," Evelyn told her. "The girls and I shall have a lovely time together. Isn't that right, you two?"

"Mmm," was Alicia's only reply, while Rose hesitated for a moment before nodding.

As soon as Evelyn wasn't looking, Rebecca slipped the last of her dandelion patties into her napkin and covered it expertly, before getting to her feet.

"Actually," she said, "I might head off now. Girls, remember to eat up all the nice breakfast you've been given."

"But -"

"It's good for you, Rose," she added, already grabbing her coat and heading to the door. "Now, if you'll excuse me, I want to follow up on a few

70

things."

***

A cold morning wind blew through the cemetery, rustling the trees as Rebecca stopped to look at the old school building. She'd seen the place plenty of times before, of course, but it had been locked up and abandoned since long before she'd been born.

"There's a ghost in there," Rose had said the night before, just before they'd all crept back into the cottage. "She's all alone."

"We heard... something," Alicia had added. "I didn't see anyone, I don't think so, but... it was quite scary."

Having promised to take a look, Rebecca was now unsure as to what her next steps should be. The idea of another haunting just dropping into her lap seemed unlikely, but as she looked at the school she had to admit that the place had a certain unnerving atmosphere that seemed to be almost leaking out. Watching the dark windows, she wondered whether Alicia and Rose had simply managed to spook themselves during the night or whether they – and Rose in particular – might in fact have picked up on something a little more substantial.

A little more real.

"Good morning."

Startled, she turned to see a man watching her from a nearby gate. Having not realized that she had any company at all, she momentarily felt a little out of sorts.

"I didn't mean to disturb you," the man continued, setting his wheelbarrow down before wiping his hands on the sides of his jacket. "We don't get too many visitors here, that's all. At least, not new faces."

Checking his hands again, he made his way over.

"It's my Saturday weeding project," he explained. "Since poor old Bob died there's been no-one to volunteer to keep the cemetery neat and tidy, so I've taken on the task myself. I don't mind, really. There's nothing like a bit of good old-fashioned hard gardening to keep us connected to the world around us."

Not really knowing how to respond, Rebecca could only offer a faint smile.

"I'm sorry, I should have introduced myself," the man continued, holding a hand out to her. "I'm Ray Rashford. Or Father Rashford, as I suppose I should say. I only recently took up my position here at Oxendon Church."

Shaking his hand, Rebecca glanced briefly at the old church.

"I was rather pensioned off, in truth," Father Rashford went on. "Sometimes, when we priests kick up a fuss about something, it's easier to ship us off to a place like this and hope we're never heard from again. Which, to be fair, is working rather well. Between gardening and all my other duties here, I barely have time to even think straight. It's a beautiful parish, it really is. But I'm sorry, I don't think I asked you, are you... just visiting?"

"My mother lives here," she explained. "Evelyn Ward?"

"Ah, yes," he said, clearly recognizing the name. "The lady who likes to search all through the cemetery for things she can eat. She was particularly happy the other week with some berries that grow over in the corner. I must say, I'm not sure that I'd like to eat such juicy rich berries, not when their roots are in the..."

His voice trailed off for a moment before he appeared to think better of finishing that sentence.

"You seemed rather transfixed by the sight of the old school," he continued, nodding in that direction. "It's a beautiful little building, although one that has been sadly untouched for many a year."

"When did it shut down?" she asked.

"Oh, fifty years ago or more. I believe that by the end, there were too few children in the village to justify the expense of keeping it open. It's always sad when something like that happens, but at the same time we must all move with the times."

"Do you know if there have been any..."

Catching herself just in time, she began to wonder whether she should really just blurt out her concerns. She'd intended to quietly and surreptitiously check the place out without attracting any attention, yet now she found herself face to face with none other than the local priest.

"I've only been inside once since I arrived," he explained, reaching into his pocket and pulling out a set of keys. "It's technically owned by the church, you see. I had some vague plan to clean the place out and try to use it as some kind of village hall, but when I suggested that idea to some of the locals... well, let's just say that my idea wasn't very well received. In fact, the reception was positively frosty."

"Why wouldn't they want it to be used?" she asked.

"Why indeed?" he replied, sorting through the keys before holding one up and stepping past her. "I really should get back to my weeding, but I'll take any opportunity for a quick break. Would you like to see inside?"

"Oh, I don't -"

"It's rather empty, but it has been left mostly untouched," he continued, already striding toward the building. "I actually should pay the place some proper attention, that idea has been in the back of my mind for a while now. I'm glad you've reminded me of it. I don't want to let the place rot forever."

"There's no need to go to any trouble for me," she told him, but he was already almost at the school's front door.

Realizing that she couldn't really back out now, Rebecca finally set off after him. The morning was already taking a few turns that she hadn't expected, although as she reached the door she at least figured that it would be good for her to check the place out properly. Alicia and Rose had seemed so freaked out by their visit during the night – Rose especially – and she couldn't quite shake the feeling that they might have stumbled upon something of note. And as she made her way closer to the old school, she couldn't help but feel a shiver run through her bones, although she quickly reminded herself that she might simply be overreacting to the rundown state of the place.

"The door can be rather stuff," Father Rashford said, struggling with the key for a moment before finally managing to get it to turn. "There we go. I knew I'd manage it eventually."

He had to force the handle too, but after a couple of attempts he managed to pull the door open. With his right foot, he pulled a rock over to prop the door open, and then he stepped aside and gestured for Rebecca to go first.

"I admit it's a rather grim sight," he continued, "but I prefer to see its potential rather than its poor current state. Please, won't you take the lead? I must warn you, though, that it's rather cold inside."

CHAPTER EIGHT

AS SHE MADE HER way along the corridor, Rebecca couldn't help but notice that her footsteps echoed loudly throughout the bare, dusty space. Reaching the far end, she looked through an open doorway and saw what had clearly once been the main classroom.

A shiver ran through her bones as she realized that Father Rashford had been right about one thing: the interior of the school was so very cold, certainly much colder than she'd expected. Reaching out, she touched the wall and felt its chill.

"It's all rather sad, isn't it?" the priest said as he headed over to the desk at the front of the old classroom. "This would have been such a happy place once, filled with the voices of children. Their absence certainly leaves a mark, doesn't it? I always think it's funny how that works. An absence can, in certain circumstances, seem more real than a presence."

"How long has the school been closed?"

"It shut its doors in 1956," he explained. "Ever since then, the children of Oxendon have had to go to the neighboring village for their early education, although to be honest there aren't many children born here. One or two a year, something like that. And they get picked up by a bus that runs through the village every morning. The council offers the service for free."

"So it was shut because it just wasn't being used enough?"

She waited for an answer, but Father Rashford conspicuously failed to elaborate as he wandered over to the window and looked outside.

"As is often the case with such things," he explained finally, "the truth is a little more complicated. The school was always manned by someone from the village, and the last teacher here was a local woman named Edith Cole. By all accounts she was much younger than her predecessors, a fact that set tongues wagging throughout the area. I suppose some of the parents worried that their children wouldn't receive a proper education from a woman barely into her early twenties, but by all accounts Miss Cole acquitted herself well and began to gain the trust of her students' parents. She became, for a time, a very popular figure in the community."

"I'm sensing that there's a twist in this tale," Rebecca told him.

"You sense correctly," he replied, still looking out the window. "There was talk of shutting the school down, of course, but it just about managed to keep going until something rather unfortunate occurred. One day in 1956, two of the last remaining students simply vanished into thin air – from this very room – and could never be found again."

"That seems unlikely."

"And yet it's what happened."

"There must have been a search."

"Oh, I'm sure there was," he said as he turned to her, "but it was one that failed to locate the children. Meredith Potter and Peter Swinson, I believe were their names. According to Miss Cole, the other children had departed for the day and young Meredith and Peter – who were aged around eight – were sitting in this very classroom while they waited to be collected by their parents."

"And then what happened?" Rebecca asked.

"Miss Cole claimed that she spoke to them briefly before going out to look for something in the storeroom. When she returned a couple of minutes later, the two children were gone. They were never seen again."

"So they left and... went off somewhere."

"Impossible. Miss Cole insisted that she would have seen them if they'd left through the main door and there's no other way in or out. And before you suggest it, the windows were found to be securely locked from the inside. Naturally a thorough search of the building was conducted, but no hiding place was ever found. To all intents and purposes, young Meredith and Peter seemed to simply blink out of existence. It seems to have been a real old mystery of the locked room variety."

"That isn't possible," Rebecca pointed out.

"Of course it isn't," he admitted, "and that's why such great suspicion fell upon poor Miss Cole. Rumors soon spread throughout the village suggesting that she knew more than she'd admitted. Questions were asked about her character and her entire private life was ripped apart. She was seen as fair game by the local community, many of whom believed that she was holding something back about the children and their true fate."

"What did the police say?"

"She was questioned, of course," he explained. "The search initially focused on the school building before expanding to include the entire village and surrounding farmland. Yet no trace of those two children was found or has ever been found since. Miss Cole retired and the school closed. My understanding is that the poor woman remained living in the village for the rest of her life but became practically a recluse. She was shunned by almost everyone around her."

"Why didn't she move away?"

"It wasn't so easy in those days," he pointed out. "And some say that she used to go out every single day still looking for the missing children. Like everyone else, she accepted that they must have died somehow, but she wanted to know how. Eventually she died without discovering the truth."

"That's horrible," Rebecca admitted, before stopping to look around the classroom. "And what about this place ever since? Have there been any... stories about it?"

"What kind of stories?"

As soon as she turned to him again, she could tell that he knew exactly what she meant.

"My daughter and the girl we're fostering were talking about this building," she told him. "Rose is a very gifted child, she seems to have a certain sympathy with the paranormal." She paused, wondering whether she was saying too much; she never knew quite how much to tell people, especially when she wasn't sure of their beliefs. "She was pretty insistent that this school building is haunted."

"Did she see something?"

She shook her head.

"There have been stories over the years," he

went on. "To be honest, I'd have been surprised if there *hadn't* been, given the nature of what happened back in the day. And I suppose having the school shuttered meant that naturally people whispered about seeing mysterious shadows at the windows, that sort of thing. All I can tell you for certain is that I have been in here multiple times in order to conduct small errands, and I have most certainly never encountered anything more terrifying than the odd spider."

"What about those children?" she asked. "They must have gone somewhere."

"Of course, but I doubt the mystery can be resolved now. Too many years have passed."

"Perhaps that would make it easier," she countered. "I'm sure emotions were running high at the time. A more dispassionate approach might help." She turned and looked around the classroom. "If the children were really in here, and if there was no other way for them to leave, then they have to have gone somewhere. And it really can't be too far, either."

As she looked around, already her mind was racing as she tried to work out where two children might have hidden – not only from their teacher, but apparently also from anyone else who tried to find them later. Had they played a simple game that had gone horribly wrong? She saw a cupboard in the corner of the room, but obviously that was far too simple a solution, so instead she tried to think outside the box. There was no obvious sign of hidden panels on the walls, but she wondered whether two inquisitive children might have found something and then became trapped. If that had happened, however, why wouldn't they have called out for help? Looking up, she saw no hint of anywhere to hide beyond the ceiling, and again that explanation seemed to raise more questions than it answered.

Yet somehow there *had* to be a clue, because – assuming that the story as told was correct – two children had apparently vanished in almost the blink of an eye.

"St. Clement's has a history of its own," Father Rashford said after a moment.

Rebecca turned to him.

"The church," he clarified. "Given my role and responsibilities, I daresay that I should be more circumspect when it comes to such matters, but... I must ask, do you have some particular interest in ghostly activity? I get the impression that you haven't merely wandered along here out of nowhere."

"My husband and I are researchers," she told him cautiously. "We've recently expanded our area of investigation to cover stories of ghosts and hauntings. Only credible stories, of course." She paused for a moment. "Not that it's easy to work out which ones are credible, at least not at the beginning. You said that the church has a history of its own. What exactly do you mean by that?"

"I mean that as a man of the cloth I should be above such things," he explained, "and that I certainly shouldn't indulge the idea that the church itself might be haunted. Unfortunately I have been here just long enough to have experienced a few things that have rather caught my attention. I really don't know whether the schoolhouse is haunted, I certainly have seen no evidence of that. But the church, on the other hand... I'm afraid that the church seems to contain something rather untoward."

CHAPTER NINE

"SAINT CLEMENT LIVED AROUND the latter half of the first century A.D.," Father Rashford explained a few minutes later, as Rebecca made her way along the nave and looked up at a large stained glass window on one side. "He was the fourth bishop of Rome and it's believed that he was martyred on the orders of Emperor Trajan."

Stopping, Rebecca looked at the colorful image that appeared to show several figures on a boat.

"If you believe the more dramatic versions of the story," Father Rashford continued, "he was thrown overboard with an anchor tied around his neck."

"Why would they do something like that?" she asked.

"Supposedly he angered the emperor and was banished to work in a stone quarry. He saw that his fellow prisoners were dying of thirst, so he followed divine intervention and located a source of water for them. Many of those prisoners subsequently converted from paganism, and for this act Clement was thrown into the Black Sea. His bones were supposedly recovered many years later in Crimea and are now housed in a basilica in Rome, although there are other versions of the story. His head, for example, is said to be interred at a monastery in the Ukrainian city of Kyiv. I've often thought that I should like to go and see his relics, but I've never quite found the time."

"And now a church is named after him in Oxendon."

"We aren't too far from the sea," he replied. "A lot of fishing families ended up here back when the sea levels were higher and the local river was more navigable. Since Saint Clement is often associated with water, I suppose it was natural that his name was invoked for... protection, I would imagine. The history is actually rather fascinating, I could bore you to death with it all day, but I imagine that's not why you followed me into the church today. You're far more interested in the ghost to which I rather subtly alluded."

"I haven't come across a ghost in a church before."

"Do you consider such a thing to be sacrilege?"

"I haven't given the matter enough thought yet," she admitted. "When you mix parapsychology and theology, the outcome might be a little muddy. I'm not sure where ghost stories end and religion begins. I feel like I'm in the deep end."

"It's wise to acknowledge the gaps in one's understanding," he said, stepping past her and approaching one side of the altar, where he stopped for a moment as his foot pressed against a slightly loose stone on the floor. "The alternative is to insist on false beliefs. That can only lead to ignorance or worse."

"Have you seen a ghost in the church, Father Rashford?"

"Hmm?" He jiggled the loose stone for a moment, as if he was playing for time, and then he met her gaze. "You'll have to forgive me. I'm finding the prospect of this conversation a little more difficult than I anticipated." He glanced up at the high ceiling. "I suddenly find myself worried about offending the boss."

"Go on," she said, unable to stifle a faint smile. "I'm sure you'll be fine."

"I believe in the word of the Lord," he told her, and now he seemed more fearful than before. "The dead face judgment and they can't come strolling back to visit the land of the living. And yet

I myself, in this exact spot, once witnessed something that chilled my blood and made me question everything I have ever thought I understood about the world."

***

"It was right here," Father Rashford continued, after a moment of uncomfortable silence, once he and Rebecca had sat in the pew at the front. "Late one night I had been here alone, completing some work, when I stopped for a few seconds of quiet contemplation."

Looking around, Rebecca saw the altar slightly to her right. The church was compact and somewhat plain, with perhaps not quite so many decorations as she remembered from similar spaces. There was a kind of leanness to the layout, as if someone had gone to great lengths to avoid any kind of ostentation, and she couldn't help but feel as if this starkness was a welcome alternative to some of the other churches she'd visited over the years. Not that she'd been to many, but there was precious little gold on display in this particular church. Having spent much of her childhood in and around Oxendon, she was surprised to realize that she had rarely been inside the church before.

"I became aware of a sound coming from the south transept," the priest said, turning and looking to the space beyond the right-hand side of the altar. "A shuffling sound, it seemed to me, as if somebody was in there. I could see it as clearly as I see it now, and I am absolutely certain that nobody was there. Yet the sound persisted for several seconds, rather brazenly going on even though I could see for myself that there were no feet moving in that space, and then it was gone."

"Pigeons?"

He turned to her.

"I know from experience," she continued, "that it's very easy to misinterpret a sound when you're... feeling a little spooked by things."

"Indeed, but the story doesn't end there," he countered. The fear in his eyes was impossible to miss and his voice had seemed to tighten a little in his throat. "I dismissed the experience, as any right-minded person would, and then I got back to work. I still had a few things to do, mainly in the chancel, but a short while later I heard the same sound again, coming from the same place. This time I marched straight through to the south transept, convinced that I would find the source of the noise, but instead it stopped abruptly just as I arrived."

"There *are* other possibles explanations," she pointed out.

"You don't need to tell me that," he replied.

"I don't mean to sound condescending."

"You do not, I assure you."

He hesitated, and she could already tell that something more was on his mind.

"But then I saw him," he added, looking over toward the spot near the altar where he'd earlier examined the loose stone. "I saw a figure dressed in black standing right there, with his back turned to me. It was the most astonishing sight, for I knew I had locked the door before beginning my work. There was no way that anyone else should have been in here with me, yet there this fellow stood, and I couldn't help but note that he seemed completely unafraid of me. In fact, it was almost as if he was daring me to notice him."

She waited for him to go on, but he seemed lost in thought.

"Did you... try to speak to him?" she asked finally.

"I asked him what he was doing, and who he was, but he completely ignored me. I began to make my way over to him but I stopped as I felt... I can't describe it exactly, but I felt a sudden sense that I should maintain my distance. It was as if I somehow understood on some... deep basic level that this was something to be avoided, perhaps even feared."

"So what did you do instead?"

"I hesitated, while I silently asked the Lord for guidance, and then the figure began to walk around past the side of the chancel."

"Did you follow?"

"At first I was too concerned about the entire situation, but then... yes, I followed. And as I went around that corner, the figure's footsteps faded to nothing and I found that there was no sign of the man. I can assure you that there was nowhere he could have gone, yet he appeared to simply fade away into thin air. I know how that sounds, Ms. Pearson, and I have not shared the story with anyone else. I merely thought that, in light of your earlier interest, I should be honest with you. But please don't spread what I have told you to anyone else."

"Of course not," she replied. "Have you experienced anything else here in the church? Has anyone else?"

"There have long been rumors," he told her. "A few whispered tales of strange sensations, but as far as I'm aware nobody has claimed to have actually seen anything here. I am the sole lucky individual in that regard."

"And you don't have any idea who the figure might have been?"

He hesitated for a moment, before shaking his head.

"I can't pretend to have an answer for you," she admitted. "Don't take this the wrong way, but as ghost stories go, that really wasn't the most shocking."

At this, he smiled.

"It's an interesting intersection, though," she added. "Ghosts and religion. My husband could probably write a whole series of papers on the subject. I've got to admit, I don't know much about how the Bible treats ghosts, but I'm sure Jonathan would be able to come up with a whole load of theories."

"The Bible teaches us that the dead do not come back to wander among the living," Father Rashford told her as he continued to stare at the spot where he'd once seen the mysterious figure. "Rather, we are told that such apparitions should be avoided." He paused again. "For they are demons."

CHAPTER TEN

"ROSE, LOOK!" ALICIA CALLED out breathlessly as she reached the fence and looked over at the field of sheep. "Rose, hurry up! There are loads of them!"

For a moment, captivated by the sight of the sheep – most of which had been marked on their sides by a spray of blue dye – Alicia could only watch with a growing smile as the animals busied themselves all across the field. Having grown up mostly in a town, she'd spent very little time out in the countryside and the sight of so many sheep seemed almost miraculous. She watched for several more seconds, lost in her surroundings, before realizing that Rose had yet to say anything.

Turning, she saw that there was no sign of Rose at all.

"Where are you?" she shouted, feeling slightly irritated by the idea that once again Rose couldn't just be normal for five seconds. "Rose?"

She waited, but she saw no hint of anyone. The spire of the Oxendon church rose up beyond a line of trees, but otherwise Alicia could almost have believed in that instant that she was the only living person in the entire world. She turned and looked around, yet the church spire was the only sign of civilization – save, of course, for the low wooden fence that separated the field from the rest of the land.

And then, just as she was about to call out again, she spotted a figure in the distance, and she realized that Rose must have stopped much earlier than she'd noticed. Sighing, she briefly considered calling out but quickly understood that there was no point. As the sheep continued to mooch around in the field, Alicia began to pick her way back through the long grass while silently wondering whether Rose was ever going to be able to act like a normal person.

***

"So what are you up to?" she asked a couple of minutes later as she finally reached the spot where Rose was standing. "Did you find something fun?"

Although she waited for an answer and gave

Rose enough time to say something, deep down she already knew that her new friend was lost in another of her strange trances.

"You and Rose are going to get along really well," she remembered her mother telling her back before Rose had first arrived. "It'll be good for you to have a friend."

That wasn't quite how things had worked out. As much as Alicia liked Rose and had tried to befriend her, there remained a certain barrier between the two girls. Sure, Alicia knew that she wasn't necessarily the best at making new friends, but she'd quickly learned that something about Rose just seemed very... different. Her father's constant experiments with the girl didn't help, yet Alicia felt that something more fundamental was 'off' about Rose, as if she didn't quite exist in the same world as everyone else. And although she felt slightly guilty for feeling that way, Alicia was starting to wonder whether she was ever going to be able to fully get through to her.

Sometimes she felt that Rose simply didn't *want* to be friends.

"Hey," she continued, before reaching out and nudging Rose's hand, "what -"

Suddenly Rose turned and glared at her.

"What?" Alicia asked, unable to hide the fact that she was taken aback by the expression in her eyes. "What's wrong?"

Rose stared for a few more seconds before turning and looking back at the treeline again. Following her gaze, Alicia realized that she appeared to be watching the distant church spire.

"It looks so small from here," Rose said after a moment, keeping her voice low. "You can still see it, though. Even when everything else is out of view, you can't miss it."

"Sure," Alicia replied, even though she didn't quite understand what Rose was talking about. "Hey, do you want to come and see the sheep? They're really cute."

As much as she wanted to get through to Rose, she already knew that she was unlikely to persuade her. Instead Rose seemed to be utterly transfixed by the sight of the distant church, and after a moment Alicia could only let out a sigh as she turned to go back over to the fence.

"Whatever," she muttered. "I only -"

"Why won't they leave me alone?" Rose added, raising her voice a little now. "Why must they always come to my place and try to interfere? Don't they understand that when they cross the threshold they're entering *my* domain? I don't seek to involve myself in their affairs so why do they think to meddle in mine?"

Stopping, Alicia turned to her again.

"What did you just say?" she asked cautiously.

"It's no good," Rose said, shaking her head sadly. "It's no good at all. Can't they see that I tried? Can't they see that I did everything in my power to avoid this? If they'd just left me alone I would have alright, and they would have been as well, but instead..."

Her voice trailed off for a few seconds, and then she turned and stared directly at Alicia again.

"Instead... what?" Alicia asked cautiously.

"What do you mean?" Rose replied.

"What were you just talking about?"

"I don't know," Rose said, "but..."

She hesitated for a moment before suddenly her knees gave way. Just as she began to fall, however, Alicia raced over and managed to catch her, and she then proceeded to help her over to a nearby tree stump so that she could sit down.

"Are you having another seizure?"

"No," Rose replied, shaking her head furiously. "Not this time."

"But -"

"I'm not," Rose said again, a little more firmly. "It feels like how it felt before, but I can control it now. I can push back and stop it taking over."

"What are you talking about now?" Alicia asked, trying not to sound too annoyed.

Looking past her, Rose saw the church spire again. She opened her mouth as if she was about to say something, but instead she remained silent as she continued to stare.

"I felt it," she whispered finally.

"Felt what?" Alicia asked. "Rose, you're starting to scare me. I think we should go and find my mum."

"No, there's no point worrying her," Rose replied. "It was only for a second, it was like I could feel someone's mind reaching out to me and... and I think it was coming from that church."

"How would a mind be doing that?"

"I don't know, but it was really powerful. It was like it was going to take over and keep talking through me, but I started to slowly feel stronger. It wasn't easy but I managed to force it back out." She paused, as if she was listening to something that Alicia couldn't hear at all. "And now it's gone. At first it was trying to get back in, but it's gone completely now and I don't think it's coming back. Not at the moment."

"You're not making any sense," Alicia pointed out.

"It was so strong," Rose continued, "and so powerful and so... determined. It felt desperate, like it had been trying to get someone to hear its voice for a long time and it was so happy that it finally found me. I don't know what it was, but it was old. But... not as old as the thing at Lotham Lodge. That was a bit older. This felt like it might have existed about a century ago or maybe a bit less."

"I'm telling Mum."

"No!" Rose blurted out. "Please don't, I don't want your dad to put more wires on me and do more of those experiments."

"But -"

"Please, Alicia," Rose continued, reaching out and grabbing her by the hand, then squeezing tight. "Not yet. Let me think about it a little bit more first. I want to work it out myself." She waited for Alicia to agree. "I really hate it when your dad makes me do those tests. At first I just found them boring, but they've started to get scary. Please, don't say anything that might make him do more of them."

"I won't say anything yet," Alicia told her cautiously, still weighing up her options and feeling more than a little troubled, "but if anything else bad happens, I'll have to. You understand that, don't you?"

Rose nodded.

"Are the tests really that bad?" Alicia asked. "I knew you didn't like them, but I didn't know you hated them so much."

"It's like he's trying to pull something out of me," Rose explained. "Something that I don't want to think about. And I'm scared about what might happen if his tests work. Why can't I just forget and live like a normal person?"

CHAPTER ELEVEN

"NO, BUT IT REMINDS me a little of Marlstone Hall," Rebecca said as she stood in the kitchen of her mother's cottage, making a cup of tea while keeping her phone tucked next to her left ear. "There are definite similarities. You've got an adult with a duty of care, and you've got something bad happening to the children they were supposed to look after."

"I'm sure it's just a coincidence," Jonathan said on the other end of the line.

"I don't know," she replied, adding some milk to the tea. "What if it's not? What if certain types of emotional state can trigger something that we don't understand yet? And Rose is a very empathetic girl, so that might be how she picked up on it all. At Marlstone Hall two years ago, Emma

Kemp's ghost was trying to put things right in regard to the children who'd died under her care. And now here at Oxendon, you've got the ghost of Edith Cole who lost two children in unusual circumstances. Even the names of the two women are quite similar."

"So what are you suggesting?"

"I'm not suggesting anything," she said with a sigh. "I'm just pointing out the similarities, really."

"The thing with the kids is easy enough to explain," he pointed out. "They ran off and the teacher just didn't want to admit that she'd left them alone for too long. Then they scurried off, the ways kids always do, and they met some tragic fate. If they fell down some kind of storm drain, for example, or into a septic tank... as horrible as the idea is, they might easily have not been found."

"I know you're right," Rebecca replied, although she certainly didn't sound convinced.

"I'm more interested in what you told me about the church," he admitted. "Assuming that this priest you met isn't a total lunatic, it's quite a surprise to hear a man of the cloth acknowledging a possible ghostly presence on hallowed ground. I would have expected someone like him to be the biggest skeptic of all."

"You don't think they're linked, do you?"

"How could they possibly be linked?"

"I don't have the first clue," she told him,

"but something's going on here, Jonathan. Something weird. I think I remember hearing the vaguest whispers about the old school building when I was a kid, but I never knew the whole story. I asked Mum about it when I got back earlier and she clearly didn't want to talk about it too much. I know communities tend to close ranks when there's a tragedy, but I find it hard to believe that no-one here ever had any idea about what actually happened to those girls."

"So are you going to turn into Miss Marple and try to figure it out?"

"Are you offering to come down here and help?"

"You know I'm snowed under," he reminded her.

"You always tend to be busy whenever I visit Mum."

"Now that *is* a coincidence," he told her. "Listen, I should get going, but I think you should probably focus on getting your mum to have that stair lift thingy installed in the cottage. She's not getting any younger, even if she thinks she can still go charging about like she did in the old days. The last thing I want is to see you having to keep going down there just because she's getting too infirm."

"I know you're right," she replied as she stirred the tea and then set the spoon on a nearby plate next to the discarded bag. "And there's probably no real mystery here. The kids went missing, and the figure in the church was probably a misunderstanding. I just can't quite bring myself to believe that there might be an actual ghost in a church at all."

Hearing a knock on the front door, she leaned into the hallway and saw a shadowy figure on the other side of the frosted glass.

"Someone's at the door," she told Jonathan. "Mum's taking a nap. I'd better go."

Once she'd cut the call, she set the phone down and placed it on the counter, and then she hurried to the front door and pulled it open.

"Hey," she said, shocked to see a familiar figure standing outside. "Can I help you with anything?"

***

"Rose!" Alicia yelled from somewhere far off in the distance, round toward the other side of the cemetery. "Come and look at this! It's so cool!"

"Coming!" Rose replied, having spent the previous few minutes examining one of the more unusual graves.

Set behind a low metal railing, one of the graves looked more like a small tomb, with a sloped roof and lettering on the side explaining that multiple members of the same family were buried within. One of the things that Rose really liked the most about old cemeteries was the fact that almost no two graves were the same; some people had been buried beneath simple stones while others had clearly wanted something much more flamboyant. The only thing that united them, she realized as she turned to follow the path around to the rear of the cemetery, was the fact that over time they'd all become faded and damaged, with cracks on their leaning surfaces and moss covering many of the words.

"Rose!" Alicia shouted. "It's the fattest cat I ever saw in my life!"

"Coming!" Rose called out again.

And then, as she passed the front of the church, she saw that the door was wide open. She felt sure that just a few minutes ago it had been shut; she'd even given it a gentle push to see whether she could look inside, but it had been firmly locked. Now, however, it seemed to have opened in complete silence, revealing a gloomy interior.

Stopping in her tracks, she looked through and saw the backs of several rows of pews.

She heard Alicia's voice calling her again, but this time the sound barely penetrated her consciousness. Instead she cautiously stepped toward the door, entering the porch area and then setting foot inside the building itself. She saw the altar at the far end, but she was far more interested in the rows of empty pews on either side of the central aisle. And although she knew she should simply turn around and leave, she couldn't shake the feeling that somehow someone was waiting for her in this space.

Stepping forward again, she put a hand on the side of one pew, feeling the mottled wood for a few seconds. She looked down and saw knee protecting pads hanging from small hooks, and then she looked toward the altar again. She wanted to call out and ask whether anyone was around, but at the last second she decided that this might be a mistake.

Instinctively taking a step back, she told herself that she should simply leave and go to Alicia. In fact, she wasn't sure that she even remembered stepping into the church in the first place.

"Well, hello there," a voice said suddenly.

Startled, she spun around and stepped back so fast that she bumped against one of the pews and lost her footing. Falling, she landed with a hard bump against the floor.

"I'm sorry," the priest said, holding both his hands up, "I didn't mean to scare you."

"The door was open!" she spluttered.

"I know," he replied with a faint, amused smile. "I'm the one who opened it."

Although she wanted to reply to him, for a moment Rose was too scared to even stand up.

"And I did that," the priest continued, "because this is a house of the Lord, and because everyone is welcome here. Can you understand that, little girl?"

Rose hesitated, and then slowly she nodded.

"Would you like me to help you up?" he asked, holding a hand out toward her.

Ignoring the hand, Rose stood without any assistance.

"I never want anyone to feel uncomfortable or unwelcome here at St. Clement's," the priest said, stepping past her and walking slowly toward the altar. His black robes were perhaps a little too long and brushed slightly against the floor. "I understand that this can be an intimidating place, though, especially for those who don't come here very often. Tell me, do your parents often bring you to services?"

"No," Rose admitted, still fighting the urge to turn and run.

"More's the pity," the priest said, stopping halfway along the aisle but keeping his back turned to her. "I always find it difficult to understand when parents deprive their children of the chance to experience the peace and calm of the church. Then again, in this terrifying modern world, it can be so very difficult to feel settled at all. Do you find that, young lady? Do you find yourself fretting about where the world is heading?"

"I don't know," Rose said nervously, worried about giving the wrong answer. "I didn't mean to come in here. I just saw that the door was open and -"

"But we've met before," the priest continued, slowly turning to look back at her, just as the door swung shut again. "I think you know exactly who I am."

CHAPTER TWELVE

"I'M SORRY TO HAVE called on you so unexpectedly like this," Father Rashford said as he took a seat in the cottage's front room. "You must be utterly sick of the sight of me, but I couldn't help thinking about our conversation this morning."

"I was just discussing the situation with my husband on the phone," Rebecca explained as she sat in an armchair in the opposite corner. "He convinced me to stop fussing too much and to just focus on dealing with things here with my mother."

She waited for the priest to reply, thinking that he was probably going to agree, but after just a few seconds she realized that he seemed almost disappointed by her answer.

"Why do I get the feeling," she continued cautiously, "that maybe you didn't tell me the whole story earlier?"

"What gave it away?"

"The sheer guilt in your face right now."

"You must understand that this is a delicate situation," he replied. "I have a responsibility to the church and while I abhor corruption and deception in all its forms, I must balance my personal feelings with the need to protect the integrity of the institution that I represent."

"Of course," she said, still trying to figure out exactly where he was coming from. She could tell already that she absolutely needed to tread carefully, but a niggling thought was gnawing away at the back of her mind – indeed, this was a thought that had originally burst unbidden into her mind while she was in the church earlier.

She swallowed hard.

"You know the figure in the church," she added finally. "I mean, you know who he is. You recognized him."

"Am I that transparent?"

"You didn't say anything about being scared," she continued. "When most people talk about encountering a ghost, the first thing they describe is the fear they felt. You didn't mention any of that."

"Ha," he said flatly. "Well observed."

"I'm not really an expert," she told him, "but that stood out to me."

"You're quite right, of course," he said with a sigh. "Even from behind, even without him saying a world, I did indeed recognize the figure. And that only made the situation stranger, because I knew full well that this particular individual was dead. In fact, I had been the one who presided over his funeral not long before the day of his rather ghostly return."

"Was he a friend?"

"Not exactly," he told her, and still he seemed reluctant to go into full detail. "He was my predecessor. He was the man I replaced when I was sent here to take over the parish of Oxendon."

***

Ten years earlier...

"Father Pottinger," Father Rashford said, standing outside the front of the church and extending a hand, "it's an honor to meet you. My name is Father Raymond Rashford and I -"

"I know who you are," the old man spat back at him, ignoring the hand and instead shuffling over to the noticeboard, which he began to unlock with a trembling hand. "I already told them, this whole thing is a waste of time. I don't need replacing."

"I wouldn't think of it quite in those terms,"

Father Rashford replied. "It's more -"

"Bus drivers retire," Father Pottinger continued, jiggling the key in the lock as his arthritic hand struggled to grip it properly. "Civil servants retire. Farmers retire. Priests do not retire."

"Indeed, but they do perhaps... transition to a more relaxed way of living. One that they have more than earned after many years of service and devotion to the church."

"Piffle!"

"I was actually thinking," Father Rashford went on, "that I would be honored if I could merely... shadow you for a few months."

"Shadow me?"

"To see how you do things. This is my first parish, and while I learned a great deal during my training, I know that there's nothing like experience in the real world. In the field, so to speak. I imagine I could learn so much from you if I could just watch you as you work."

He waited for a reply, but Father Pottinger was clearly ignoring him and seemed to be focused instead on the business of trying to turn the key in the lock. Although he could see that the man's hands were shaking badly, Father Rashford felt that it would be rather rude of him to simply step over and try to intervene, so he decided instead to wait for a suitable juncture so that Father Pottinger might accept that *asking* for help was by far the better approach.

"Damn thing," the old man hissed, rattling the noticeboard's door with a little more force than before. "I swear someone comes along sometimes and gums up the works. It's sabotage, that's what it is! They're probably laughing at me!"

"Father Pottinger -"

"They think it's funny to watch an old man and his struggles. Well, I'll show them. I might be old but I know what I'm doing, and I'm not going to be dissuaded by some foolish children and their pathetic games."

"Father Pottinger -"

"The Devil gets into their minds and persuades them to think up their little tricks! It's the Devil, I tell you all, and it might start like this but soon it escalates and becomes something far worse. Even the purest of minds must keep their guards up at all times, lest the Devil might sneak his way in, because after that it's almost impossible to get the bastard out. I tell them this all the time, but do they listen? Sometimes I think that my words fall upon deaf ears."

"Father Pottinger -"

"What do you want?" he shouted angrily, turning to Father Rashford just as the key snapped in the lock. "Damn and blast it, now look what you've made me do!"

"I'm truly sorry," Father Rashford replied,

"but I must confess I was told that you might be reticent to accept the fact of my arrival."

"What are you blathering on about now?"

"I'm simply trying to impress upon you the fact that I have been sent to take over the parish of Oxendon," Father Rashford continued, "and that this new arrangement is not up for negotiation. Indeed I was told that you have been informed multiple times that I would be arriving today, even if you have not replied to most of those messages. Father, I am not for one moment trying to push you out of the way, but I think it's important to drive home the point that I *am* going to be taking up my new position."

"I'm going to need a locksmith," Father Pottinger muttered, taking a step back from the noticeboard. "Now I can't put up any posters for a day or two. How are people going to know what's going on?"

"Does the church have a website?"

At this suggestion, Father Pottinger turned and glared at him.

"If I might take a look," Father Rashford said, stepping over to the noticeboard and taking a set of keys from his pocket, then using a tool on the chain to fiddle with the lock. "This is a very simple system," he said as he wiggled the broken part of the key out before opening the noticeboard's two doors and turning to Father Pottinger with a rather satisfied expression. "See? It really didn't require much work at all. We can get a new key made, although it's barely a key at all. It's more of a... simple piece of metal, actually."

"Huh," Father Pottinger replied, clearly unimpressed.

"So the problem is solved."

"Hmm."

"As I mentioned," Father Rashford said, slipping his own keys away before once again holding his hand out, "my name is Father Rashford but people call me Raymond, sometimes even Ray. I'm truly looking forward to my time here at Oxendon and I really can't wait to get to know the local area. I've got to admit, though, that I'm a little lost right now, so I could use a guided tour. When you have a spare moment, would you possibly be able to show me around?"

"Show you around?"

"Not that I want to be a bother, though. I just -"

"I'll be needing a locksmith," Father Pottinger said, turning and heading back toward the church's front door. "It's not good having a noticeboard that any Tom, Dick or Sally can open. Why, I need to have full control over that thing. The time has come to fit a proper lock."

"Is that strictly necessary?" Father Rashford asked, turning to watch as the old man disappeared into the church.

Left standing all alone, the younger priest looked around for a moment. So far his impression of Oxendon was highly favorable, although he had to admit that his welcome from the irascible Father Pottinger had been significantly less pleasant than he'd been expecting. Still, he told himself that this was only one meeting, and that first impressions could surely be overcome with a little time and perseverance.

CHAPTER THIRTEEN

"THIS IS A FINE old church," Father Rashford said many hours later, sitting in one of the front pews once darkness had begun to fall outside. "The photographs really didn't do it justice, although I must confess, it's a little on the chilly side."

By this point he wasn't really expecting much of an answer, and sure enough he simply heard Father Pottinger bumping around somewhere in the chancel. Having been warned that Frank Pottinger wasn't exactly renowned for his good humor, Father Rashford had braced himself for trouble, but so far he was mostly being ignored. At the same time, he fully understood the elderly gentleman's reasons for being so difficult; no priest ever liked to be pensioned off, even if most of them put on a brave face and at least pretended to be looking forward to retirement.

A moment later Father Pottinger made his way back into view, carrying a chair. Although his first instinct was to offer some help, Father Rashford knew from experience that any such offer would only make the situation far worse. Diplomacy, he reminded himself, was the order of the day.

"I said that this is a fine old church," he continued instead, trying to at least get a conversation started. "I think I shall come to like it here a great deal."

After setting the chair down, Father Pottinger turned to return to the chancel, before stopping suddenly with his back turned. It was this view that Father Rashford would see again many years later, following the elderly man's death and burial.

"And there will always be a place here for you in the church, Father Pottinger," he continued. "Should you choose to remain living in Oxendon, you will always have a huge role to play in the life of the parish."

He waited, but now Father Pottinger seemed almost frozen in place.

"Are you a good man?" the elderly priest asked finally, his voice descending to almost a growl now. "I don't mean do you do good things, I mean... deep down, in your heart, do you know yourself to be a good man?"

"I certainly hope so."

"That's not what I asked!" Father Pottinger barked, with his back still turned. "Listen, you damn fool! I asked you whether you're a good man through and through. It should be an easy enough question to answer!"

Before he could proffer a response, Father Rashford thought back once more to some words of advice that had been given to him by another priest – one who had known Father Pottinger for many years.

"His mind is shot," the priest had explained, with great sadness in his voice. "It's such a tragedy. He refuses to see a doctor, but he's got... I don't know if it's dementia or Alzheimer's or something else, but he can't go on like this. He used to have a brilliant mind but those days are long gone. Someone has to gently move him aside."

"I try every single day to be the best person I can be," Father Rashford said finally. "Whether that is enough to make me a 'good man', I shall leave the decision to others. I certainly do not go around announcing myself as one, for therein would be complacency and arrogance."

"Pfft!" Father Pottinger spluttered, shaking his head. "A non-committal answer if ever I heard one. Why are you so wishy washy? You shouldn't be so afraid to -"

Suddenly he turned, as if he'd heard something nearby – and in the process a bone clicked in his neck. Father Rashford tried to follow his gaze, but he saw only the empty pews in front of the altar. He waited , convinced that the elderly man would brush the whole thing off, yet after a few seconds he realized that something seemed to be very wrong.

"Father Pottinger?" he said cautiously. "Is anything the matter?"

"I don't know what they want," Father Pottinger whispered, his voice barely loud enough now for anyone else to hear. "I don't remember..."

"What don't you remember?" Father Rashford asked.

At that question, Father Pottinger turned to him, and for a few seconds the old man's eyes appeared slightly milky. After a couple of seconds more, a solitary tear began to run from one of those eyes, making its way down his cheek and leaving a glistening trail.

"Who did you say you are again?" Father Pottinger stammered finally. "I'm sorry, I... I seem to have lost my train of thought."

"I -"

"Damn it!" the old man continued, suddenly getting to his feet. "I can't sit around here all day! I've got work to do!"

With that, he shuffled away along the aisle,

still muttering to himself. Left sitting alone, Father Rashford tried to make sense of everything that was happening, before finally rising as he realized that he needed to keep up.

***

"Vandals!" Father Pottinger snarled, slamming the noticeboard's doors shut with anger. "Look at it! What kind of person would damage a church noticeboard? What is the world coming to?"

Finally catching up to him, Father Rashford was about to remind him that he – Father Pottinger – had broken the key just a short while earlier, but at the last second he realized that there was no point. The old man was clearly struggling with his memory, unable to remember very much at all, and there was a certain sadness in the way that he now stood staring helplessly at the broken lock.

"What... what kind of person... what kind of person would do this?"

"Perhaps we should go inside," Father Rashford said firmly, keenly aware now that his task was going to be much more difficult than he'd previously understood. "It's cold and it's getting late, and I rather think that we need to discuss a few matters."

"Hmm?"

For a moment this information seemed not

to have made its way into the old man's mind at all, until finally he turned and glared at Father Rashford.

"Who are you?" he barked.

"I arrived this morning," Father Rashford reminded him, hoping to nudge his memory. "We have been discussing a few issues relating to my impending role here in the parish. I am going to be taking on your duties and responsibilities and -"

"Nonsense!" Father Pottinger spat back at him. "Are you a madman? Why would I need anyone to take on my duties and responsibilities? I'm the only person who knows how things work around here! There's not another soul in the world who could do half of what I do! Who are you *really*? Have you been sent to test me?"

"I have all the relevant documentation to show you. I also know that you were contacted previously on several occasions and specifically warned that I would be -"

"Warned? About what?"

"That I shall be assuming the role of priest in this parish."

"But *I'm* the priest!"

"You are to be moved into a more... advisory role."

"What the hell are you going on about now?" Father Pottinger hissed. "You're a fool, that's what you are! You've obviously got the wrong end of the stick about something, that's for sure! I've got a good few years left in me yet, I won't be shoved out of the way just because some pen pushing idiot hundreds of miles away sees a number on a piece of paper and decides that I'm too old. I'm fine, I get everything done, I..."

Turning to look at the noticeboard, he seemed momentarily transfixed by the sight of the lock. His mouth hung open slightly as if he was on the verge of saying – or perhaps remembering – something, yet now he seemed to be almost frozen in place.

"I know this won't be easy," Father Rashford said after several more seconds had passed. "I would very much like to sit down and discuss the matter with you properly. Perhaps over a cup of tea?"

"They're damned annoying, that's what they are," Father Pottinger replied.

"I beg your -"

"Why won't they go away? If you want to make yourself useful, why don't you start by doing that, eh? Make them... shut up and leave me alone! I don't know who they are and I don't know what they want!"

He began to shuffle back along the path, heading toward the church once more.

"It's not right. I don't know where their parents are, but someone ought to take those children in hand and teach them some basic respect!"

"What children?" Father Rashford asked, turning to watch as the old man walked away. "Father Pottinger? There are no children here! If you tell me exactly what is troubling you, I can try to help, but I'm afraid I'm going to need a little more guidance."

He waited, but in truth he could already tell that he wasn't going to get an answer. Although he'd been warned to expect certain difficulties when dealing with Father Pottinger, he now realized that the situation was far more awkward that he'd been led to believe; indeed, he worried that he might be wholly unqualified for the task of managing his predecessor's departure. At the same time, he had never shied away from a tough task, so he told himself that he was simply going to have to dig deeper and find the right words.

Already, as he stood by the noticeboard, he realized that he could still hear Father Pottinger talking to himself inside the church.

CHAPTER FOURTEEN

Ten years later...

"ARE YOU SURE IT was him?" Rebecca asked once Father Rashford had finished telling her about Father Pottinger. "You might have been mistaken or -"

"No, it was him," the priest replied. "Trust me, I would not be making this admission had I not spent many hours struggling with my thoughts on the matter. If even a scintilla of doubt existed, I would keep my mouth shut and not express my concerns to anyone."

He hesitated, as if he was scared to say more.

"I saw Father Pottinger's ghost," he added. "It's really as simply as that. You must think that I'm out of my mind."

"Not for one second," she told him. "It sounds like he wasn't... malevolent. He didn't seem to try to contact you in any way, either."

"Yet he appeared before me. That must mean something."

"Did it only happen the one time?"

He nodded.

"I've got to confess that I'm far from an expert in these matters," she admitted. "My husband and I have started to look into aspects of the paranormal much more seriously, but we're still at the very beginning of our work. I'm not completely sure that I'm in any position to offer you advice."

"Although I haven't seen the spectral figure since," Father Rashford said cautiously, "I have quite often felt a kind of... presence. You are the first person I've ever spoken to about the matter, but it's as if – at times – I can tell that someone is near me."

"In the church?"

"Always. And always around the spot where I once saw him."

"That must be significant."

"And you and your husband... have seen actual ghosts before?"

"I encountered something a couple of years ago," she explained, "and then last year my husband was involved in an incident at a house. I know that's not a huge amount of experience, but it has been enough to persuade us both that there's something worth looking into. But I need to emphasize that we're both very much amateurs at the moment. I'm afraid I don't know of any magic way to get rid of a ghost."

"If Father Pottinger is lingering in the church, does that mean that he has some form of... unfinished business?"

"It might well do."

"By the end of his life, his memory was utterly ruined," he continued. "His short term memory was almost non-existent and the long term wasn't much better. He had a few older memories, but the poor man's mind was filled with holes. I spent a great deal of time with him at the end and I saw the absolute terror in his eyes. I could just never quite work out what was causing that terror. Was it something he remembered, or might it have been something he'd forgotten?"

***

"I... I've never seen you before," Rose said softly, watching as the priest slowly made his way along the aisle, heading toward the altar. "I have to go now."

Turning, she hurried back the way she'd come and tried to get the door open, only to find that for some reason it was now stubbornly locked. She pulled a couple more times, yet if anything the lock seemed to become stronger. The metal section rattled a few times, and then she stopped just in time to hear the priest's footsteps ringing out at the far end of the space.

Looking over her shoulder, she saw that he was now facing the altar. Coming to a standstill, he stood with his back to her.

"I don't know who you are," she whispered.

"Come now," he replied, and his voice echoed slightly beneath the high vaulted ceiling. "For one so young, you have much intelligence in your eyes – and a certain amount of sympathy for these things, I perceive. I think you know very much that we have met before."

She shook her head.

"When you were in one of the fields earlier," he continued, "I reached out and felt your mind. You can't have missed that."

"Are you..."

Her voice trailed off for a moment. She very much wanted to leave the church, yet somehow she felt drawn to the strange man. Stepping forward, she began to make her way slowly along the aisle even though her heart was pounding and she felt fear crawling its way up over her ribs.

"Yes?" the man replied, sounding slightly amused by her reticence.

"Are you... a ghost?" she asked.

"What an unusual question," he replied, half turning to her – just enough to reveal a smile on his lips. "Do you expect a straight answer? If I can *state* that I am dead, does that not mean that there is some... slippage between the two conditions? How can a dead man even speak to you?"

"Are you a priest?"

"I was the priest here once, before I was rudely pushed aside. The unfortunate thing is that at the end of my days, I was suffering from an inability to recall everything from my life. Now that I am... past that condition, I am better able to remember things. It is as if I have reverted to my last good self. So I must say that your question just now was hopelessly naive. You should not have asked me whether I am a ghost."

He turned to her.

"You should have asked me *which* ghost I am."

"I... don't know what you mean," she stammered, trying to hide her fear.

"Am I the ghost of who I was when I died? Am I the ghost of that feeble old man on his death bed? Or am I the ghost of the same man when he was younger, when he was in his prime?"

"I don't know," she admitted.

"It is a strange thing to forget much of one's own life," he said calmly. "To have holes in your memory, to know that they're there but to be unable to get past them. The inner world disappears, leaving only ghosts within one's own thoughts."

"I should go," Rose said, not really understanding what the man was saying as she took a step back.

"Ghosts within ghosts," he snarled, "nested like Russian dolls. I used to wrestle endlessly with the question of whether or not I was a good man. The truth is, I was a *very* good man almost entirely through my life. But I struggled desperately with dark, evil thoughts. For almost all of my life, however, I was able to push those thoughts out of my mind and focus on being the best man possible. And yet..."

He took one step forward.

The stone beneath his left foot shifted slightly.

"And yet," he continued, "I was weak for just one brief moment. Mere seconds, really. I let my guard down and allowed the worst of myself to emerge. And by the time I had forced myself to be good again, I had already caused such harm."

"I should go," Rose said again, turning and heading back to the door.

Pulling harder and harder, she realized that she was starting to panic. She wanted Alicia to show up and help her, but in that moment she could only think about the fact that she *had* to get out of the church. A moment later, however, she turned and looked back toward the alter – and she saw to her immense relief that the strange priest was now gone. She glanced around, but she saw no sign of him anywhere.

Trying the door again, however, she found that it was still locked. She did everything she could think of to lift the latch, yet somehow the entire door remained firmly in place.

"Please let me out," she whimpered as tears began to fill her eyes. "Alicia, can you hear me? Are you out there? Alicia, what -"

Suddenly she froze as she felt a hand touching her shoulder from behind. She already knew somehow that this hand belonged to the strange priest, but she couldn't bring herself to turn and look at him. Instead she stared straight ahead at the door even though she knew that it wouldn't open, and she told herself that hopefully the priest would simply leave her alone.

"One moment," he snarled. "One brief moment in an otherwise perfect life. Is that really enough to consign a man to the depths of Hell? I was so good, I fought against everything that burned in my heart, and I only slipped once. Must I pay for that now? Must I suffer for all eternity?"

"I just want to leave," she whispered, and now her voice was trembling with fear.

"It's not fair!" he hissed. "I was a good man!

Why must I pay for one mistake?"

"Please let me go," she said, forcing herself to turn and look up at him. "Please, I only -"

In that moment she saw that his features were paler than before and that the flesh was clinging to his skull, and that his eyes had sunk so deep that they resembled nothing more than two dark, smoky pits glaring back down at her. She wanted to run, or to try to talk to him or to be brave, but she could do none of those things.

She could only scream.

CHAPTER FIFTEEN

"HEY," REBECCA SAID AS she and Father Rashford stepped into the cemetery and saw Alicia hitting a bush with a long stick. "What are you girls up to?"

"I don't know," Alicia said mournfully. "I think Rose is hiding from me."

"What do you mean?"

"I can't find her. She won't answer when I call her name."

"How long has it been since you saw her?"

"I don't know. Ten minutes, maybe. But she just -"

Suddenly a scream rang out, breaking the tranquil silence of the cemetery.

"I think that's coming from inside," Father Rashford stammered.

Racing around to the front of the church, Rebecca tried to get the door open, only to find that it was locked. She could hear Rose still screaming inside, however, along with what sounded like a series of loud bumps.

"Rose, open the door!" she yelled. "Rose, can you hear me? I'm right here, I need you to open the door!"

"There's another way in!" Father Rashford shouted, already racing past her and hurrying down the side of the building.

Rushing after him, Rebecca quickly saw that he was opening a small wooden door. She raced into the church and overtook him, making her way through a small side room before emerging into one of the transepts just as Rose's scream faded to nothing. For a moment, filled with a sense of panic, she looked all around yet still she saw no sign of the girl.

"Rose?" she shouted. "Where are you?"

She stopped and looked all around. She couldn't see any hint of Rose's presence at all, but a few seconds later she heard a frantic scrabbling sound. Walking past the pews, she tried to follow the sound and finally she spotted Rose crawling quickly across the floor as if she was trying to get away from someone or something.

"It's okay, Rose," she said, hurrying over and reaching down to grab her by the arm. "What -"

"Get away from me!" Rose shouted, pushing her away. "Leave me alone!"

"Rose, it's me!" Rebecca hissed, taking hold of both her arms and forcing her to look up. "Rose, listen to me. Rose, it's okay, I'm here! Rose, I -"

Before she could finish, Rose lashed out and struck the side of her mouth with a fist. Wincing, Rebecca pulled back and touched her lip; seeing blood on her fingertip, she quickly reminded herself that Rose was simply panicking.

"Rose, I need you to focus," she said firmly, grabbing the girl's arm again. "It's me. Rose, look at me!"

Although she opened her mouth to cry out, Rose finally seemed to realize what was happening. She stared up at Rebecca for a few seconds before turning just as she saw Father Rashford making his way over, and then she looked back toward the church's main door.

"He's gone," she whispered.

"Who's gone?" Rebecca asked.

"The scary priest," Rose said, turning to her again with tears in her eyes. "He was chasing me. I think he wanted to hurt me."

***

"Is this him?"

Holding up the photo, which showed him

standing with Father Pottinger, Father Rashford waited for Rose to answer. Having retreated to Evelyn's cottage, they were all sitting in the front room now as Rose stared at the old newspaper page announcing Father Pottinger's retirement.

She narrowed her eyes slightly.

"No," she said finally.

"No?" Father Rashford replied, unable to hide a sense of disappointment.

"Wait," Rose said, taking the piece of paper and moving it closer so that she could study it more carefully. "Yes. I think so. He was different, though."

"In what way?" Rebecca asked, dabbing at the cut on her lip with a tissue.

"He was younger."

"Are you sure?"

Rose stared at the photo for a few more seconds before holding it back out and nodding.

"That was the same person," she said, "but he was much younger. He looks really old in the photo but in the church he was about your age."

"*My* age?" Rebecca replied.

"I'm really sorry about your lip," Rose added sheepishly. "I didn't mean to hit you."

"That would have been long before I ever came to Oxendon," Father Rashford pointed out. "Father Pottinger was here for most of his life, however. I believe he was something like twenty-five or so when he first set foot in the parish."

"But I thought ghosts -"

Stopping herself just in time, Rebecca tried to make sense of everything that was happening.

"I thought," she continued cautiously, "that ghosts were frozen in the form of the person when they died. If Father Pottinger died as an old man, how can his ghost be younger?"

"You're the expert," Father Rashford replied.

"Far from it," she admitted. "Then again, from what you told me, it sounds like Father Pottinger was barely even himself by the time he died. What if the ghost has taken the form he was in at the most important moment in his life? Or the most impactful?"

"Or the moment that most clearly defined him," Father Rashford suggested. "For better or for worse."

"He was saying all these strange things that didn't make sense," Rose told them, sniffing back a few more tears. "He seemed really angry about something."

"I don't doubt that," Rebecca replied, reaching over and tousling the hair on top of her head for a moment. "The important thing is that you're safe now. Just promise me that you won't go back into that church, okay? At least not without me."

"What about the teacher?" Alicia asked.

The others turned to her.

"Are there two ghosts here?" the young girl continued. "One in the school and one in the church?"

"It looks that way," Rebecca told her.

"Then do they... do they know each other?"

"Father Pottinger was here in the parish when Edith Cole was teaching," Father Pottinger told her. "In fact, he would have been here when all the unfortunate business happened with those two children who vanished. As such, I imagine that their lives would have overlapped a great deal. For example, he would have been involved in the search, and he would also have provided counsel and help to poor Edith."

"She was vilified by the community, wasn't she?" Rebecca asked.

He nodded.

"Do you happen to know," she continued, "what Father Pottinger's opinion was on the matter?"

"Not his private opinion," Father Rashford replied, "but I have no doubt that he would have set aside any ill feelings toward the poor woman so that he could instead help her. That, after all, would have been part of his role. He certainly wouldn't have tried to judge her."

"How can you be so sure?"

"It's part of our training," he explained.

"Many's the time when someone comes and confesses to something shocking, but as priests we must set aside our personal reactions and focus on helping that soul to overcome their difficulties. That might sound impossible to some people, and I admit that it's hard sometimes, but... I hesitate to use a word such as 'professional', but I suppose in a way that's what I mean. I have had people from this very village come to me and confess to terrible things, yet I dealt with them in the manner that my training taught me."

"That's admirable," Rebecca told him, "but you can't be sure that Father Pottinger was the same. Still, it's not necessarily too important. These might well be two entirely separate hauntings."

"They're just a hundred meters or so apart."

"That doesn't have to mean anything," she continued. "I'm pretty sure that ghosts don't hang out and chat to each other. And both the church and the school building are places where you might expect some kind of spirit to linger. I think it's really important that we refrain from seeing connections that don't actually exist. Otherwise we risk coming up with all these crazy theories that have almost no basis in reality."

"Perhaps," he said, before reaching into his pocket and pulling out another newspaper clipping, this time one that was faded and clearly much older. Holding it up, he showed it to Rose. "I very deliberately saved this one for second. Rose, is -"

"That's him!" she blurted out before he had a chance to finish. "That's the priest from the church! That's exactly what he looked like!"

"Are you sure?" he asked.

She nodded.

"This is important," he continued. "Rose, are you really sure? When you saw the ghost, did anything about him seem in any way either older or younger?"

She shook her head.

"You're certain?"

"That's him," she stammered. "That's *exactly* what he looked like."

"This newspaper clipping is from the opening of a local fete in 1956," Father Rashford explained, turning to Rebecca. "The same year in which young Meredith Potter and Peter Swinson disappeared from Edith Cole's classroom. So, Mrs. Pearson, do you still believe that the two ghosts aren't connected?"

CHAPTER SIXTEEN

STANDING ON TIPTOES IN the cottage's cramped dining room, Alicia tried to ignore the voices drifting through from the front room as she looked at various old framed photos. She saw several faces in the images, but so far she didn't recognize any of them at all.

"That's your grandfather."

Startled, she turned to see that her grandmother had made her way through.

"They're talking about ghosts," Evelyn continued with a faint smile. "Not really my favorite topic. And not yours either, I suspect."

Wandering over, she took down one of the photos, which showed a handsome young man in an RAF uniform.

"He died the same year you were born," she

explained. "Your parents got married a little earlier than planned so that he'd be able to walk your mother down the aisle. Poor Tom, he was so sick by then but he was determined – absolutely determined – to be there for the big day. I truly believe that he refused to die any earlier, that sheer force of will got him through to the wedding. If that sounds silly, I don't care. You know, sometimes you remind me of him a little."

"I do?"

Evelyn nodded.

"How?" Alicia asked, staring at the photo. "We don't look the same."

"It's more about your personalities," Evelyn told her. "Tom was quite a quiet man, he usually didn't say much unless he was spoken to. But I loved that about him, because – as you must have noticed – I can rather natter my head off if I'm given even half a chance. I suppose you could say that we complemented one another perfectly."

"What does that mean?"

"It means that sometimes I did the talking when he wasn't saying enough, and then at other times he gently reminded me that I was allowed to... take a moment to catch my breath."

Alicia smiled.

"You know," Evelyn added, "I've got something that you might like. In fact, it might only be a little bit too big for you now. You can grow into it. Hold on a moment."

Shuffling across the room, she opened the door to a cupboard in the corner and started rifling through various old coats, before pulling out what appeared to be some kind of camouflage jacket.

"This was his," she explained, carrying it back over. "He was given it during his time in the air force, and he used to wear it long after he'd retired. His other jackets from those days are long gone, but this one..."

She set it over Alicia's shoulders.

"Well, it's slightly too big for you," she continued as the girl slipped her arms into the sleeves, "but as I said, you've got plenty of time to grow into it. Do you want it?"

"Are you sure?" Alicia asked as she examined the jacket more carefully.

"I think Tom would be pleased to know that someone's using it," Evelyn told her as tears began to glisten slightly in her eyes. "And it suits you. I honestly can't believe how much you remind me of him, Alicia. It's almost like seeing a ghost."

Reaching out, she pulled her granddaughter closer and hugged her tight.

"You're a good girl," she continued, kissing the top of her head. "Just promise me that you'll look after your granddad's old jacket, okay? Don't lose it or give it away to anyone."

"Of course not," Alicia replied with a smile.

"Thank you, Nana. I love it. I'm going to keep it for the rest of my life!"

***

As she stood on the grassy roadside beyond the front of the cottage, Rebecca watched as the setting sun slowly cast both the church and the distant school in dark shadows.

"So let me get this straight," Jonathan said over the phone. "You think these two situations are linked somehow?"

"That seems to be the case," she murmured.

She waited for him to reply, but after a few seconds she simply heard a sigh.

"You think I'm barking up the wrong tree," she added.

"I didn't say that."

"I can hear it in your tone."

"I don't have a tone," he insisted. "I'm just... struggling to get my head around it all. If the ghost in the church and the ghost in the school are linked somehow, that's... unlike any of the other situations we've encountered so far."

"Is it?" she asked. "The ghost of the gamekeeper and Lord Makepeace at Lotham Lodge seemed to be pretty intertwined. It's almost as if one of them couldn't exist without the other. What if the same thing is going on here? Father Pottinger seems to have returned to haunt the church in the exact form he had when those children went missing. Which, from what Father Rashford has told me, is a period of his own life that he barely remembered by the time he was older. Both the ghosts appear to be rooted in those events from 1956."

"So what's the plan?"

"I keep thinking about the children," she admitted. "Kids can't simply vanish from a room."

"Agreed, but you don't know that this Edith woman was a reliable witness. Sure, she claims that they couldn't have left without her seeing, but what if she was just trying to cover up the fact that she took her eye off the ball?"

"Apparently she kept insisting that she'd done her job properly right up until the end," she reminded him. "If she was lying, don't you think that eventually she would have admitted it?"

"Not necessarily."

"I think she was telling the truth," she said firmly, "at least as far as she understood it."

"So what happened to the two children? Did they fall through a trapdoor in the floor? Did they get sucked up into a vent? Did a U.F.O. land and take them away?"

"More importantly," she replied, "did they ever actually leave the school?"

"What are you suggesting?"

"That if there's no way they *could* have

left... they must still be there somewhere. Or at least, their bones must be. What if that's what this whole mess is all about? At the heart of it, the ghosts of the two missing children just want to be found so that they can be buried properly."

"That sounds pretty cliched."

"All the ghosts we've encountered so far have had some kind of unfinished business," she reminded him. "The ghost of Edith Cole wants to find out what happened to the children. The ghosts of Meredith Potter and Peter Swinson want to have their remains found. And then that just leaves Father Pottinger, who seems to have completely lost his mind by the time he was dying. But back in the day, back in 1956, he might have somehow been connected to the disappearance."

"The trope of the evil priest, huh?"

"I'm going to spend the night in the school," she announced suddenly.

"Alone?"

"I'll be fine."

"Absolutely not," he said firmly. "Rebecca, are you crazy? Do you remember what happened to me at Lotham Lodge last year? I could have died!"

"But -"

"It's out of the question," he continued. "Listen, how about this for a compromise? When you get back, we'll study this whole situation from a scientific standpoint. We'll analyze it properly and come up with theories, and then we'll develop methods of testing those theories. And then, *if* we make sufficient progress, there's nothing stopping us going to Oxendon again in six months or so and running some rigorous, controlled tests. That's the only way for us to ever get any answers."

"I'm already here," she pointed out. "What's the harm in me taking a look?"

"I got attacked by ghost deer," he reminded her. "Who knows what else is possible?"

"Fine," she said, unable to hide a sense of frustration as she saw that the sun had sunk lower, filling the horizon with various shades of red and yellow. "I know you're right, it's just frustrating that the answer might be right there and we have no way of getting to it."

"We agreed to approach our investigations carefully," he pointed out. "Now isn't the time to rush in like a bull in a china shop."

"I know you're right," she said as she heard the front door opening, and she turned to see her mother emerging from the cottage. "Listen, I'll call you back later, okay?"

Once she'd cut the call, she waited as Evelyn made her way over.

"I gave Alicia one of your father's old jackets," Evelyn said. "I suppose I'm just being sentimental, but it seemed like the right thing to do, somehow. And it suits her!"

"They're similar in so many ways."

"That's what I said!"

Rebecca hesitated, still watching the dark silhouettes of the buildings in the distance, and already she could feel a plan forming in the back of her mind. She hated the idea of lying, but more than that she hated the idea of missing a golden opportunity to get to the truth.

"Mum," she said finally, "would you mind watching the girls tonight while I go out?"

"Off to meet some friends?"

"Not quite," she admitted. "I'm going to stake out that old school building. Jonathan thinks it's dangerous, but I'm certain that he's wrong. I just need to find out what's going on in that place once and for all. You don't think I'm being too gung ho, do you?"

"I wouldn't have it any other way," Evelyn said with a smile. "Of course I'll watch the girls. I like Jonathan, but he can be terribly timid sometimes." She patted her daughter on the shoulder. "I know you'll be fine in there. Just try to get some decent photos of the ghosts, okay? None of that blurry, out of focus rubbish that people usually try to pass off on people."

CHAPTER SEVENTEEN

"NO, IT'S ABSOLUTELY FINE," Father Rashford said as he sat at the desk in his study, with his mobile phone resting in front of him. "We can reschedule the bric-a-brac sale. Pushing it back a week won't really make much difference, will it?"

"You'd be surprised how much fuss some people make," Malcolm Waters said over the line. "If you change the routine in any way at all, they come out of the woodwork waving their handbags and insisting that we're breaking ancient traditions."

"Village life will survive a one week postponement of the bric-a-brac sale," Father Rashford insisted, unable to stifle a slight smile. "If anyone has any complaints, feel free to direct them to me and I'll explain the situation. We need to make as much money as possible for the church's repairs.

The leak in the roof is getting worse and those damaged stones on the floor are becoming a real hazard."

"Yes, I noticed that as well," Malcolm mused. "That floor was only fixed a few decades ago. Back in the 1950s, I think. It shouldn't be causing trouble again so soon."

"These things are sent to test us," Father Rashford pointed out, glancing at the window and seeing the church about a hundred feet away across the cemetery. "One must always remember to -"

Before he was able to finish, he spotted a hint of movement in a window at the rear of the building. This particular window looked into the small office that had been built many years after the rest of the church, but he'd personally locked the place up about one hour earlier and he knew that there absolutely shouldn't be anybody in there at all.

"Father Rashford?" Malcolm said after a few more seconds had passed. "Were you about to say something?"

"Let's proceed as you see fit," he replied. "I'm sorry, Malcolm, something has come up. I hope you don't mind if we end this call a little prematurely. It's just that I think I need to go and attend to another matter."

Once the call was over, he made his way to the window and looked out once more at the church. His heart was racing and although he was trying to convince himself that there was no need to worry, he felt absolutely sure that he'd seen a distinct shape briefly moving inside the church's office. He told himself that there was no reason to believe that a ghostly presence had returned, yet this only led to more worry as he realized that perhaps some vandal might have broken into the building. Whichever way he looked at the situation, he knew that he had a duty to go and take a look, so finally he checked in his pocket to make sure that he still had the key.

"I'm sure it's nothing," he said under his breath, in an attempt to calm his raging nerves. "I'm sure it's just... a trick of the light."

***

"No, I'm not going to get another burger!" Rebecca hissed, before turning to look out at the landing for a moment, to make sure that there was no way anyone could be eavesdropping.

After a moment she turned to look back at Alicia, who was tucked up in bed.

"I told you, I'm going to do a little... investigating. That's all."

"But -"

"And I need you to keep it to yourself," she added, glancing at the empty bed on the other side of the room.

She could hear running water coming from

the bathroom and she knew that Rose would be through soon, so she figured that she had to work fast.

"Normally I'd never encourage you to deceive anyone," she continued, "but I need to make sure that Rose doesn't get... worked up. That's why I don't want her to know that I'm going to the school. If she notices that I've gone out, just tell her that I've gone to see an old friend."

"Are you sure you'll be okay over there?" Alicia asked.

"I'll be fine," she said, leaning down and kissing her daughter's forehead as she heard the toilet flushing. "The only danger is that I might catch a cold. I don't think there's any heating in that place."

As Rose made her way through, Rebecca pulled the duvet from the other bed and helped her to get in, and then she gave the girl a kiss on the cheek.

"I want you both to be really good and go straight to sleep, okay?" she continued as she got to her feet. "You've had a busy day and tomorrow we'll be getting up nice and early. We're going to have lunch at a nice little pub nearby, but first I want use to make room for the food by having a long walk. Does that sound like a good idea?"

"Yes," both girls replied somewhat unenthusiastically.

"That's the spirit," Rebecca said as she headed to the door. "Don't worry, you'll love it. It's not hilly or anything like that. Not so much, anyway."

"Are you going somewhere?" Rose asked.

Stopping, Rebecca turned to her.

"You are," Rose continued.

"What makes you say that?"

"You've still got your shoes on," Rose pointed out. "You find the buckle annoying to open and close, so you keep them on if you think you're going somewhere again soon. If you weren't going out, you'd have taken them off for dinner but instead -"

"Alright, Sherlock," Rebecca said, interrupting her. "As it happens, yes, I'm going to see an old friend."

"I thought you said -"

"I have friends, you know," Rebecca continued before the girl could get another word out. "Don't worry, I won't be too long, but I'll be back slightly late so I want you both to be asleep by then. I'll be checking on you so don't let me down."

"Okay," Alicia said.

Rose hesitated, fixing Rebecca with a determined stare for a few seconds longer.

"Okay," she added finally.

Once Rebecca had left the room and had bumped the door shut, Rose continued to stare into darkness. Alicia rolled over onto one side, meanwhile, and spent several minutes with her eyes closed as she tried to get to sleep. Finally admitting defeat, however, she opened her eyes again and saw the shadows of nearby trees casting dark shapes against the window, and in the back of her mind she was already fairly sure that Rose wasn't asleep at all.

She didn't want to turn and look, of course, because she worried that she'd only end up giving Rose more ammunition. She continued to watch the window, then, even as she realized that she felt more awake than ever. A couple of minutes later she heard the front door shutting, followed by the sound of her mother's footsteps walking away across the gravel. As much as she hated the idea of anyone going to that spooky old school at night, she told herself that her mother knew what she was doing and that everything was going to be fine.

After a few more minutes, realizing that she hadn't heard so much as a pin drop in the room, she began to think that perhaps Rose had fallen asleep after all. She still didn't want to turn and look, yet she couldn't shake an overwhelming need to at least confirm her hope, and finally she understood that she was going to have to check. She continued to watch the window for a few more seconds, letting the silence of the room settle a little more, and then she very slowly started to roll over so that she could look at the other bed.

"Where's she really going?" Rose asked, towering over her.

Startled, Alicia let out a shocked gasp as she pulled back against the wall.

"She's not going to see a friend," Rose continued, "because last week at dinner she told Jonathan that she doesn't have any friends round here anymore, and also her car keys were in the bowl downstairs after dinner and I didn't hear her pick them up, and also she left a few minutes ago but she didn't turn the car's engine on. So she's obviously not going to meet friends, which means she lied, and the only reason she'd lie would be if she doesn't want us – or me – to know where she's really going."

"Do you *ever* stop?" Alicia asked.

"Stop what?"

"Being weird!"

Sighing, Alicia sat up a little more in the bed.

"She's gone to the school, hasn't she?" Rose added. "It's okay, I know she probably swore you to secrecy so I won't make you feel bad by asking again. I *know* she's gone to the school, because that's where I'd go if I was her. It makes sense and to be honest, I'd be worried if she didn't go. But if she hasn't told me, then I'm guessing she hasn't told your father either, and I can't help but feel a bit worried about her."

"She... she said she'd be fine," Alicia stammered.

"But she might be wrong," Rose pointed out, before turning and looking over at the door for a moment. "Your grandma's gone to sleep already," she added. "I can hear her snoring. That means the coast is clear and we can go to make sure that your mum's okay." She turned to Alicia again. "I don't think we should let her be in there alone."

CHAPTER EIGHTEEN

THE WIRE TWITCHED SLIGHTLY, the tension bar turned, and finally the lock on the school door clicked open. As soon as she was sure that her little trick had worked, Rebecca pulled both pieces of metal out and placed them into her pocket, while slipping inside and then pushing the door shut again.

As soon as she was in the school's corridor, she noticed how much colder the space had become. Shivering slightly, she looked into the darkness and waited for her eyes to adjust, but after a few seconds she realized that there was simply too little light. With clouds covering the moon, the entire school was shrouded in darkness. While Rebecca had planned to get around without using any kind of torch, she realized now that this would be impossible, so she told herself that she was simply going to have to hope that she didn't get caught.

She could have told Father Rashford about her plans, of course, but she'd worried that he might try to join her in the investigation, and – for some reason that she couldn't quite put her finger on – she felt as if she was going to have better luck if she worked alone.

Stepping along the corridor, she slipped her phone out and activated the flashlight. This granted her a bright but small pool of light, one that she quickly found wasn't very useful for long distances. As she reached an open doorway, for example, she held the flashlight up but saw little more than the door itself and part of the wall beyond. Tilting the phone slightly, she saw that the shadows moved at an alarming pace, but she was starting to realize that she perhaps hadn't planned the night too well.

Then again, she also realized that none of those fears really mattered. All that mattered was finding out how the two children had vanished all those years ago.

After making her way into the main classroom – with her footsteps ringing out loudly in the otherwise deathly silent space – she looked at the old desks. She wasn't sure exactly where young Meredith and Peter had sat all those years earlier, but there were only a dozen desks so she reasoned that it wouldn't take long for her to check the room properly. She began by walking past each desk in turn while glancing around in the hope that she might spot some hidden crack that might conceal the bodies of the two children, but deep down she knew that the mystery was likely to be a little harder to crack.

Once she'd checked all the desks, she began to do the same with the walls, floor and ceiling. She was still convinced that the children must have somehow found their way into a narrow space, and that then – for whatever reason – they'd been unable to call for help. Quite why nobody had ever found them, she wasn't sure, but already her theory was starting to fall apart as she realized that there were no secret panels anywhere. Stopping for a moment, she looked around the room again and saw the windows, but she already knew from Father Rashford's account of the story that Edith claimed the windows had been locked.

"Where did you go?" she whispered, before considering another possibility. "What about *you*, Edith? Did you lie about what really happened that day?"

***

1956...

Humming to herself, Edith Cole set the pile of

prayer books down before taking a moment to clear a space on one of the shelves in the school's little storeroom. Once that was done, she placed the prayer books in their proper spot and then stood back to admire her work so far.

At the end of another long day, she felt a little tired but she was already thinking about her plans for the following morning. She was often left to devise her own activities for the children, and she took her responsibilities seriously. Now she was thinking that she might teach them about Britain in the time of the Romans, which meant that she was going to have to spend the evening swotting up on the basic facts. Fortunately she already had a decent book on the subject at home, and she loved nothing more than a little light research.

Sighing, she turned and headed out into the corridor, only to let out a shocked gasp as she saw Meredith Potter and Peter Swinson – two of the children from her class – standing just inside the doorway.

"Heavens, you gave me such a start!" she exclaimed. "School is over for the day. What's wrong, can't you go home? Are your parents out?"

"Can we wait here for a little while?" Meredith asked cautiously.

"You really shouldn't," Edith replied. "School is over and ordinarily I would have already locked up, but I'm just doing some rearranging."

"Can we wait while you do that?" Meredith continued.

"I can't exactly throw you out into the cold, can I?" Edith muttered with a sigh, before gesturing for them to follow her along to the classroom. "You'll have to be very well-behaved, though, and I'll have no hesitation in casting you out if you cause trouble. Is that clear?"

"Yes, Miss Cole," Peter said.

"I'm afraid I don't have anything for you to do," Edith explained as she stopped in the classroom and watched the two children heading to a couple of desks. "This is all very irregular, but you'll simply have to sit there until I'm done. And then, if your parents still aren't home... I have to ask, where are they? Peter, your father always finishes at the mill in the early afternoon. Where are he and your mother?"

"We think they're out," Meredith said before Peter could answer for himself.

"And what about *your* parents?" Edith continued.

"They must be out too, I suppose," Meredith replied. "We're sorry, Miss Cole, we don't want you to be angry with us. If you want us to leave, we can."

"Heavens, no," Edith muttered. "Just sit down and... and find some way to amuse yourselves. In fact, in a minute or two I might have a job that you can do. Some of the older books need arranging. Do you think you'd like to do that?"

"We would," Meredith said, "very much, but -"

"Let me fetch them," Edith added, turning and heading back to the storeroom, murmuring away to herself now as she sorted through some books. "Just one moment!" she called back to the children as she glanced at the doorway that led out into the corridor. "In fact, do you want to come and give me a hand? Come along, children, and fetch some of the books so that you can sort them. Remember, the Devil makes work for idle hands!"

She pulled a couple more books out, before hesitating as she realized that she could hear no sound of approaching footsteps.

"Children?"

She waited, before rolling her eyes as she carried a pile of books back through to the classroom. She was accustomed to the fact that some of the children in her class could be a little lazy, although she'd always had both Meredith and Peter pegged as two of the more obliging pupils. In fact, she considered them to be two of her absolute favorites.

"You really must buck up your ideas a little," she told them as she entered. "It does nobody any good if you just -"

Stopping suddenly, she saw that all the

desks were now bare and unattended, and that there was absolutely no sign of either Meredith or Peter.

"Children?" she said again, wondering where they could possibly have gone.

Stepping forward, she heard a cracking sound and felt a floorboard creaking beneath her feet.

"You can't have gone out through the front door," she said under her breath. "I would have seen you."

She took another step forward, and another floorboard gently shifted under the pressure.

"Children?" she called out for a third time. "I'm really too busy and too tired for any foolishness, so will you please make yourselves known at once? Children, where are you?"

Hearing no reply, she headed over to the windows but – as she'd expected – she found that they were all still locked from the inside. She checked any other conceivable hiding place, yet it was as if both Meredith and Peter had vanished into thin air. Standing all alone in the classroom, she tried to think of any other way that they could possibly have departed, yet she knew the school well enough to understand that there was simply no other way. Finally, however, she told herself that she really didn't need to waste time speculating about the actions of two foolish children.

"You probably think that this is funny," she

murmured, taking one last look around before going back to the storeroom so that she could get on with her work. "Well, we'll see how funny you find it in the morning when you're forced to explain yourselves to the rest of the class."

She worked for another forty-five minutes or so, until she was disturbed by the arrival of Meredith's mother, who wondered why her daughter hadn't yet returned from school. And then, just as Edith was trying to get to the bottom of that particular mystery, Peter's mother also showed up with the same question. Slowly, over the next few hours, the nightmare became greater and greater – and Edith Cole's entire world began to very slowly collapse.

CHAPTER NINETEEN

57 years later...

THE HANDLE OF THE stationary cupboard stuck a little, briefly refusing to open at all, before Rebecca gave it a harder shove. As the door swung open, she aimed the flashlight's beam inside, but all she found was a bare space with no obvious hiding place.

Reaching out, she pushed at the interior walls, but already she could tell that there were no secret compartments. The idea of two children squirreling themselves away via such a small place was obviously absurd, yet Rebecca knew that she'd exhausted all the likely possibilities and anything she now discovered would by its very nature have to be highly implausible. Whatever had happened must, she reasoned, have been highly unusual.

Yet the children had vanished, and she couldn't shake the idea that their bones were hidden somewhere in the school.

"What did you get up to in here?" she whispered under her breath as she closed the cupboard and looked back across the classroom. "Why didn't you even call for help?"

She waited in the hope that some astonishing new possibility might leap into her mind, and then she lowered the flashlight and turned to look over at the windows. As much as she'd intended to tear the school apart in her hunt for the children, and as deeply as she'd promised herself that she wasn't going to rest until she came up with an answer, she was starting to understand that there might well be limits to her abilities.

More than half a century had passed since the children had vanished. How many people over the years must have searched for them? How, she realized now, could she expect to magically do a better job?

And then, just as she was coming around to the idea that perhaps she should head back to her mother's cottage, she heard a brief but very clear bumping sound, as if something in one of the other rooms had fallen to the floor.

"Hello?" she called out, wondering whether

someone might have followed her into the building.

Making her way back out into the corridor, she checked the door but found that it was still shut. As far as she knew, only Father Rashford had a key, so there was clearly no way that anyone else could have broken in; she'd learned her lock-picking techniques years earlier during a long and somewhat dull summer, but she felt sure that neither Alicia or Rose had gained any similar skills. She knew that she'd heard *something*, however, so she stood in silence and shone the flashlight's beam all around until finally she spotted the culprit.

A book had fallen onto the floor of a nearby room, landing with its pages spread wide open. Making her way into the room, she picked the book up and found that it contained various prayers. Clearly quite old, the book appeared to be in danger of falling apart, and when she looked at the shelves she saw a few more copies of the same title.

A moment later a large, spindly-legged spider crawled along the edge of the shelf.

"I don't think you're quite strong enough to have knocked this off," Rebecca muttered. "Still, you might have seen whoever did. I don't suppose you can -"

Suddenly she heard a bang coming from one of the other rooms, as if someone had slammed a door. Darting back out into the corridor, still holding the prayer book, she immediately saw the door leading into the classroom and somehow she knew – on some instinctive level – that the bang had rang out from that room in particular. Her heart was racing now and she told herself to stay calm, but she was already feeling more and more certain that she had company in the little school building.

"Edith Cole, is that you?" she said, even though the question made her feel a little foolish.

Heading to the doorway, she shone the flashlight at the desk but saw no sign of anyone. Lowering the beam, she began to turn away, but at the last second she saw a figure sitting slumped at the desk. She spun back around and aimed the beam again, yet now the figure was gone.

"Who's there?" she asked, trying to stay calm while just about resisting the urge to race out of the building. "Identify yourself! I want to know who you are!"

She waited, and then she began to slowly lower the flashlight once more. She couldn't see anything much at all now, except for the faintest outline of the windows on the other side of the pitch black room, but she was starting to wonder whether somehow the light had been driving the ghostly figure away. And the longer she stood in the doorway, the more she began to slowly notice the faintest hint of a chair creaking somewhere straight ahead.

Someone right next to the desk.

"Hello?" she said again, more convinced than ever now that she had company. "Is... is anyone there?"

She stared into the dark void.

"Hello?" she said for a third – fourth? – time as she felt her heart pounding. "Is anyone there?"

Again she waited, but just as she was about to ask yet again, she heard the distinctive sound of a chair leg very slowly scraping against the wooden floorboards. Although she couldn't see anything that was happening in the room directly in front of her, she was absolutely certain now that somebody had been sitting at the desk and was now slowly standing up.

***

"This way!" Rose called out, hurrying away from the cottage and immediately making her way toward the steps that led up into the cemetery. "I don't want to leave her alone for too long."

"Wait!" Alicia hissed, struggling along the stone path. Having not even stopped to put on shoes, she was walking barefoot and some of the sharper stones were constantly digging into her soles. "Rose, slow down!"

Ahead, however, Rose showed no sign whatsoever of heeding that request.

As she reached the bottom of the steps,

Alicia had to stop for a moment to get her breath back. At least she had her grandfather's old jacket now, which gave her some warmth. She could already feel a hint of stitch in her left side and she was amazed that Rose could run so fast; she knew she had to catch up but for a few seconds she could only lean against the wall as she turned and looked back along the street.

And then she saw them.

Two silhouettes were standing about a hundred feet away, and even from that distance Alicia could tell that they were two children and that they were staring straight in her direction. She waited for them to go away, but instead she felt more and more with each passing second that their eyes were fixed on her. More than that, however, was the sense that they wanted something, that they were waiting for her to realize what she was supposed to do next.

"Alicia!"

Startled, she looked up the steps and saw that Rose had returned to the top.

"Are you scared?" Rose continued.

"I can see two children," Alicia stammered.

"What?"

"Two children."

She looked along the street again; the children were still standing in the road.

"They're looking at me," she explained. "I

170

think they want something."

"We have to get to Rebecca," Rose replied, turning and hurrying away again. "We can worry about everyone else later. Come on!"

Although she knew that Rose was probably right – that Rose was seemingly *always* right when it came to the paranormal – Alicia couldn't quite bring herself to ignore the sight of the two children. She wanted to go after Rose, but instead she began to walk away from the steps, making her way through the cold night air as she felt herself almost drawn toward the mysterious figures.

"H... hello?" she said cautiously, and she saw her own breath in the air now. "Are you okay there?"

She knew she should turn around, but she couldn't help herself. The children were still staring at her but they were showing no other sign that they'd even noticed her presence. As she edged closer, however, Alicia began to make out their faces in the darkness and she realized that they looked terribly sad and mournful. By the time she got to within a few feet of them, she was unable to shake the sense that these two children were somehow not quite from the real world, as if they stood out somehow.

"What do you want?" she asked finally, once she'd summoned enough courage and dared to speak. "Do you... do you know something about what's happening?"

"He forgot about us," the boy replied calmly.

"Who are you talking about?"

"He forgot about all the awful things he did," the girl added. "He looked at us like he'd never seen us before."

"I don't know what you mean," Alicia told them. "Do you want something or... or can I go and find Rose?"

"We want him to remember," the girl continued, and now there was a hint of real anger in her voice. "We want him to pay."

"Who?" Alicia replied. "I don't know what you're talking about. I don't know who you -"

Suddenly the two children ran straight at her. Although she turned to avoid them, she wasn't fast enough – but the children didn't slam into her at all; instead they passed straight through her and she heard a pair of light sighs ringing in her ears as she lost her footing and fell, slamming down against the road.

CHAPTER TWENTY

PUSHING OPEN THE DOOR, Father Ray Rashford looked into the church and listened. He wasn't even sure what to expect, but he'd seen someone at one of the windows and he worried that an intruder might have broken into the building.

Either that, or...

"Is anyone here?" he called out, trying to sound as commanding as possible. "This is a house of the Lord and trespassers will not be tolerated. If there is anyone here, you..."

His voice trailed off as he realized that nobody had broken in. Deep down, as he'd made his way over to the church, he'd already understood what was happening.

What had *always* been happening.

As much as he wanted to turn around and go

home, instead he stepped inside and made his way to the final row of pews, and there he waited for some hint of a presence.

"I know it's you," he said finally. "Father Pottinger, I only want to help. I tried to ignore your presence, but Mrs. Pearson... well, let's just say that she has woken me up to a few realities. I know you're here, and I know that must mean that your soul is in turmoil. Please, allow me to help you."

He waited, and then he began to walk slowly along the aisle. He glanced left and right, watching for any sign of a ghostly figure sitting on one of the pews, although he supposed that Father Pottinger's spectral form most likely wouldn't show up quite so easily.

"When I first met you," he continued, "you were an old man. Your mind was riddled with holes. You came to barely even remember your own name. But I could tell..."

His voice trailed off for a moment as he continued to walk along the aisle, and as his footsteps rang out in the cold dark space. With each passing second he expected to see some sign of movement or to hear even the faintest whisper of a voice.

"I could tell that something was troubling you," he added. "Something that you perhaps didn't even remember, at least not fully. It was as if you were haunted by the ghost of some terrible memory.

Some unknown fear or guilt was tugging at you and torturing your soul. And even if you couldn't recall the details, there was no doubting the fact that you sensed a kind of -"

In that moment the door slammed shut. Startled, Father Rashford turned and looked back; he felt a growing sense of fear rising through his chest, but he knew he couldn't walk away.

Not now.

Not when the soul of Father Pottinger was so evidently in need of salvation.

"I tried to help you before," he explained. "In truth, I didn't know exactly what was wrong, but I could tell that something was troubling you. I tried, in my own way, to tease the nature of the problem out, but eventually I came to realize that you yourself were uncertain. I don't know if you remember, but I was there with you when you died and I saw the fear in your eyes. You kept whispering that you were sure you were going to be damned for all eternity, even if you didn't seem to know why. And then -"

In that instant he heard something metallic falling onto the floor. He turned and looked toward one of the transepts; although he saw no sign of anyone, he felt certain now that the ghostly form of Father Pottinger must be somewhere around.

"Ten long years have passed since you drew your final breath," he pointed out, unaware that the ghostly priest was now slowly stepping up behind him. "What is it about your life that keeps you trapped here in so much pain?"

***

Still staring into the darkness of the classroom, Rebecca listened to the soft – almost imperceptible – sound of fabric shifting. She knew full well that a figure had just risen from the chair behind the desk, and although she could see nothing at all, she was unable to ignore the fear that Edith Cole's ghost was now present.

"My... my name is Rebecca Pearson," she said, hoping that by introducing herself again she might get some kind of response. "I don't mean you any harm. In fact, I'm here to help you. I just -"

"Do you have them?" a sharp, angry voice snarled.

"Do I have what?"

"The children," the voice continued, seemingly hanging in the cold dark air all around. "Do *you* know where they went?"

"No, I don't," Rebecca replied, and she couldn't shake a sense of horrified wonder as she realized that she was actually talking to a ghost. "That's what I'm here to try to find out, actually. I can't imagine what it was like for you to -"

"Nobody believes me," the voice said,

interrupting her. "Sometimes I just want them to spit it out. I want them to tell me what they *think* I did with them. Instead I have to listen to their snide insinuations."

"The children have to have gone somewhere," Rebecca told her. "If you're certain that they couldn't have left the school, then that means they have to still be here somewhere."

She waited, but she heard nothing save for – a few seconds later – the sound of fabric rustling again.

"There must be some kind of logic to the situation," she continued. "Two young children can't simply vanish, never to be seen again."

"Yet they did. And I was a pariah for the rest of my days."

"We can fix that," Rebecca told her. "Isn't that what you want? To repair you reputation?"

"I care nothing for my reputation," the voice replied, and now she sounded truly sorrowful. "I care only for the children. That is all I have *ever* cared about. I have long since known that for my failure, I shall burn in Hell."

"Miss Cole -"

"First, though," she added, "I must save the children. Then I shall accept whatever fate is due to me."

"Did you hurt the children?" Rebecca asked. She waited.

Again, she heard only the rustling of fabric.

"I'm sorry to have to ask you that," she continued, "but you must understand that I need to rule out all the possibilities. If something happened and you're scared to admit it, the time has come to be completely honest."

"You think I would hurt them?" the voice replied. "You think I *could* hurt them?"

"I think accidents happen," Rebecca replied, fumbling for her phone as she glanced down and tried to activate the recording app. She knew her chances of success were slim, but she desperately wanted to record the conversation so that she might be able to play it back for Jonathan later. "I think people have good reasons sometimes for hiding the truth. Before we go on, Miss Cole, I just need to be sure... is there anything else you think I should know about that day?"

After a moment she managed to get the app recording, and then she waited for an answer.

"Miss Cole?" she continued, worried that she might have scared the ghostly woman away.

She waited for a few more seconds, and then she held the phone up and let its beam pick out the desk ahead. Bracing herself to see the dead figure, she was surprised to find herself staring at an empty room.

"Miss Cole?" she called out. "Edith Cole, if you can hear me, I'm sorry if I scared you away. I didn't mean to be so blunt, I was only trying to get to the bottom of everything."

She took a step forward, and in that moment her right foot pushed against another loose floorboard that let out a yawning creak.

"I believe," she continued, "that together we can figure this out once and for all. We can work out where Meredith and Peter went. You want that, don't you? After all this time, wouldn't you like to be at peace?"

She turned, shining the flashlight's beam all around, but she was starting to worry that she'd somehow managed to sever whatever connection she'd previously established with Edith Cole's ghost.

"Please come back," she added, before shutting off the recording app and bringing up Jonathan's number instead.

Tapping to dial, she waited for him to answer, but her call was quickly put through to voicemail instead.

"Damn it," she muttered, almost hanging up before figuring that she might as well leave him a message. "Jonathan, it's me," she continued, trying to work out how to concisely explain the situation. "Listen, do you have any idea how -"

Suddenly an icy hand grabbed face from behind, pulling her back and slamming her against the wall. Knocked out cold, Rebecca slumped down and her phone skidded away across the floor. A moment later silence returned as the phone's bright screen burned in the darkness, showing that the line was still connected to Jonathan's voicemail service.

CHAPTER TWENTY-ONE

"ALICIA? ALICIA, WAKE UP!"

Opening her eyes, Alicia found that she was on her side, resting on the road. She stared at the grass verge for a moment, barely able to make it out properly, before looking up and seeing her grandmother leaning over her. For a few seconds the sight was so strange, so bizarre, that she couldn't quite grasp how it had come about. She could only stare as she tried to make sense of the all the jumbled memories that lay scattered throughout her mind.

"What are you doing out here?" Evelyn gasped. "Alicia, what if a car had come along? You'd have been killed!"

"I saw -"

"What?" Evelyn asked, clearly exasperated.

She quickly looked both ways along the road again. "Alicia, can you please tell me what's going on out here?"

"I saw..."

Sitting up, Alicia looked at the spot where the children had been standing, but now there was nobody in sight. She turned and looked the other way, but she was more and more certain now that she and her grandmother were the only people out on the street so late at night. And after a few seconds she remembered the sensation of the two ghostly children literally running straight through her, and a shudder briefly passed along her bones.

"I woke up and realized that you and Rose were gone," Evelyn continued as she helped Alicia to her feet. "With your mother still out, I absolutely panicked – and then I looked out the window and I saw you here. Alicia, what in the name of all that's holy were you thinking? I know this is a quiet village, but people still use the road and -"

"Where's Rose?" Alicia asked suddenly.

"That's what *I* want to know too."

"She went up to the church," Alicia said, turning and hurrying toward the steps. "Nana, we have to find her! We have to make sure that she's okay!"

"Wait a moment," Evelyn said, struggling to keep up with her granddaughter. "Slow down. I'm not a spring chicken, you know. What exactly are you doing out here?"

"Rose thinks Mum's in danger."

"Your mother's visiting friends," Evelyn replied, reaching the bottom of the steps and looking up to see Alicia already getting to the top. "Isn't she?"

"She told me the truth," Alicia replied. "It's only Rose who wasn't supposed to know."

"Oh, right," Evelyn muttered. "I can't keep up with all these deceptions."

"I know she's checking out the school," Alicia said, looking back down at her. "She wanted to find out once and for all whether or not there's anything scary in there. She said not to worry and that she'd be fine, but Rose thinks something's really wrong."

"Hold on a moment," Evelyn muttered, taking hold of the handrail as she began to make her way up the steps. "It's so late. None of us should be out at such a dreadful time of the night, and especially not rushing around so fast. Alicia, you'll catch your death of cold."

"Granddad's jacket's keeping me warm."

"I suppose," Evelyn said, already a little breathless as she reached the top. "Now, what *exactly* did you say your mother was up to, again? I thought I'd always taught her to be careful but -"

Before she could finish, they both heard a sudden cry ringing out from the church – although the cry was quickly and abruptly cut off before it could reach a natural conclusion.

"Who was that?" Evelyn gasped.

"I don't know," Alicia replied as the panic finally took over her entire body, "but Mum might be in there! We have to help her!"

***

After pushing on the church's front door several times, Alicia finally managed to force it open just as her grandmother caught up to her. Rushing forward, the girl looked along the dark aisle but saw no sign of anyone. She waited, however, convinced that at any moment something would reveal itself.

"Mum?" she called out after a few more seconds. Her voice echoed in the church's huge space. "Are you in here?"

"I thought you said... didn't you say she went to the school?" Evelyn asked as she stepped through after her.

"But Rose came *here*," Alicia replied. "I think. I don't know. Gran, it's so confusing. I can't work out whether or not the -"

Suddenly hearing a gasp, she rushed along the aisle. As she got to the far end, she was shocked to see Father Rashford slowly sitting up and rubbing one side of his head.

"Is my mum here?" she asked.

"Your mother?"

Looking up at her, Father Rashford seemed momentarily confused as he continued to touch the sore spot just next to his left ear.

"I'm afraid I don't know where she is," he admitted. "I came in here to investigate the source of a strange noise, and then something..."

Looking back across the church, he seemed to be watching in case somebody else showed up.

"There was someone in here with me," he continued as he very unsteadily got to his feet. "I didn't quite get a proper look at their face, I'm afraid, but they managed to throw me clear across several rows of the pews. I can't imagine who might be that strong, unless..."

He turned first to Alicia and then to Evelyn.

"Unless they were, perhaps, not entirely of this world."

"What are you talking about?" Evelyn asked, clearly flustered by his comments. "Father Rashford, I've never heard you talking like this before. You don't seriously think that there's anything amiss in here, do you?"

"A few days ago I would have dismissed the whole idea out of hand," he murmured, "yet something seems to be stirring here right now. I'm more certain than ever that the spirit of Father Pottinger seems to be roaming this place, yet I still can't work out what might be troubling him. Young

Rose described him as a younger man, so it would seem that in his spirit-form he has somehow regressed to an earlier version of himself. How is that even possible?"

"The undead are a kind of distillation of who they truly were when they were alive," Evelyn suggested.

Alicia and Father Rashford turned to her.

"That has always been my assumption, at least," she continued, as if she was surprised by their surprise. "What? Do you think that if I come back as a ghost, I want to be an old lady? I'd much rather come back looking how I did back in my thirties, and perhaps haunting somewhere nicer like the South of France. I spent a lot of time down there when I was younger and I got to know some of the most famous movie stars of the 1970s." She took a moment to adjust her hair. "I'll have you know that I was quite the looker back then. Why, I had relationships with two award-winning American actors who -"

"Gran," Alicia said, interrupting her, "do you think we can talk about this later?"

"I'm just pointing out," Evelyn continued, "that just because someone's old when they die, that doesn't necessarily mean that they're old as a ghost. What if they come back in the version of their existence that most... sums up their struggles? Or the version they prefer?"

Alicia opened her mouth to reply.

"I think your grandmother might be absolutely correct," Father Pottinger said firmly. "But if that's the case, then why has Father Pottinger returned in his 1950s form? What happened back then that somehow became the very essence of his soul?"

Before anyone could answer, they all heard a loud clattering sound coming from somewhere nearby.

"I think it was through here," Father Pottinger said, hurrying past the altar. "Alicia, I think you had better stay back where it's safe."

"Yes, stay here," Evelyn added, stepping past her granddaughter and setting off in pursuit of the priest. "I must say, this has rather perked me up now. I'm feeling more awake than ever!"

"Why do *I* have to stay behind?" Alicia complained, but both adults had already disappeared from view.

Left standing all alone, she looked around but saw nothing except rows and rows of empty pews. Something about the church seemed extremely unsettling to her in that moment, although she couldn't quite put her finger on the cause of that sensation. As the hairs began to stir on the back of her neck, however, she couldn't help continually looking around until finally she took an involuntary step back, only for a stone on the floor to slip beneath her left foot.

Startled, she turned again and looked down, only just managing to stay standing as she saw that one of the stones had slipped fully out of place to reveal a muddy and somewhat dark gaping hole beneath.

Leaning down, she looked at the gap and tried to work out exactly what she was seeing. She had no idea whether or not churches had basements – or weren't they called crypts? - but the space certainly seemed to be quite large. Dropping to her knees, she looked even more closely at the gap before reaching her hand down into the hole and immediately feeling a faint cold breeze. She opened her mouth to call out to her grandmother and the priest, yet for a few more seconds she found herself gazing into the hole almost as if she was hypnotized.

"Alicia, it's okay!" Evelyn called out from somewhere far ahead. "Come and see!"

Alicia looked up.

Suddenly a pale, partially rotten hand darted up from beneath the hole and grabbed her by the throat, instantly squeezing so tight that she could only let out the faintest cry for help.

CHAPTER TWENTY-TWO

"AND NOW," THE VOICE on the television said as Jonathan wandered out of the front room and made his way toward the kitchen, "it's time for live figure-skating from the -"

Unable to hear more of the announcement as he turned the kitchen light on and made his way to the fridge, he couldn't help but wonder why he was still awake. Unaccustomed to having the house all to himself, he felt as if he should in some way try to make full use of the situation, yet in truth he was tired and he wanted nothing more than to go to bed. Still, he told himself that at just thirty-nine years of age he really shouldn't be retiring so early – and that he should find some way to really enjoy himself.

Opening the fridge, he looked inside and saw some beers, but he realized after a moment that he actually just wanted a nice soothing cup of caffeine-free tea.

"Damn it," he murmured under his breath "When did I become so... old?"

As he shut the fridge door, he spotted something blinking on the bench. Walking over, he realized that he'd left his phone behind when he'd gone through to watch the television, and now he had a voicemail message. Unlocking the screen, he saw that the message had been sent by Rebecca a short while earlier, so he tapped to play it back as he returned to the fridge.

"Jonathan, it's me," Rebecca's voice said, sounding somewhat tense as he reached for the water filter jug. "Listen, do you have any idea how -"

He pulled the jug out and set it down, just as he heard a faint bumping sound on the message. Looking at the phone, he furrowed his brow as he realized that Rebecca had apparently stopped talking halfway through a sentence. He could just about hear a faint hissing noise, however, so as far as he could tell the message was still being recorded. And then, slowly, he realized that he could also hear another voice coming from the phone's speakers.

Walking back over, he picked the phone up and set the volume to maximum so that he might be able to hear the second voice better.

"You have no idea," a woman's faint, rasping voice was saying, "how long I've waited to find them. *He* took them! I know he did! I just have to work out how!"

Hearing a thud, as if something had hit a wall, Jonathan tilted his head slightly as the message continued.

"He will take another," the voice added, "and -"

"End of message," the phone company's automated announcer said suddenly. "To listen to the message again, press one. To delete the message, press -"

Tapping the number one, Jonathan listened to the message for a second time, then for a third and a fourth. Each time he hoped to come to some moment of sudden realization, yet each time the second – stranger and more rasping – voice simply sounded more and more unreal. Finally he cut the call and tried to ring Rebecca back, but the phone rang for about one minute before going through to *her* voicemail.

"Rebecca, hey, it's me," he said cautiously, trying to avoid a sense of terror. "Listen, that last message you left for me just now was pretty weird. I'm not going to overreact just yet, but can you call me back as soon as possible? I just... want to make sure that everything's okay."

He hesitated before cutting the call, and then

– after setting the phone down – he waited for a moment longer. He kept telling himself that everything was going to be alright, yet for some reason in the pit of his belly a sense of genuine dread was slowly starting to form.

***

"What the..."

As soon as she opened her eyes, Rebecca felt a pounding, pulsing pain on the back of her head. She was cold, almost shivering, and it took a few seconds before she even remembered that she was in the old school. Slowly sitting up, she winced as the pain became a little stronger, but after a few more seconds she realized that something had grabbed her from behind and had slammed her head against the wall.

Suddenly letting out a gasp, she pulled back until she bumped into the side of a desk, and then she looked ahead into the darkness and waited for even the slightest noise.

Instead, all she heard was silence.

"Hello?" she said cautiously, and she was immediately shocked by the fear in her own voice. "Is anyone there?"

She waited, but now she was starting to think – to hope, really – that she might actually be alone. Certainly there was no hint of a presence nearby, at least not at first, although after a few more seconds she began to wonder whether she could feel something watching her.

"Is there anyone here?" she continued. "Is... is there anyone here named Edith Cole? I think I met you earlier. My name is Rebecca Pearson and I swear that I'm only trying to help."

Again she waited, but she heard nothing – not even the sound of rustling fabric that she'd noticed before. A few seconds later, however, a light briefly blinked on the floor just ahead.

Reaching out, she found her phone and pulled it closer, and when she looked at the screen she saw that she had a missed call and a voicemail message from Jonathan. Despite the pain in her head, she tapped to check the voicemail and then she waited for the call to connect.

"Rebecca, hey, it's me," Jonathan's voice said suddenly. "Listen, that last message you left for me just now was pretty weird. I'm not going to overreact just yet, but can you call me back as soon as possible? I just... want to make sure that everything's okay."

Puzzled, she checked her call log and saw that she had indeed tried to call him, although she felt fairly sure that she'd been knocked out before she'd managed to speak to him. Her thoughts were still a little groggy and she wasn't quite sure what to tell her husband, but she quickly brought his number up and figured that he might be able to give her some advice.

And then she froze as she realized that she could hear the rustling fabric again.

Slowly turning to look across the room, she was just about able to make out the desk at the far end, and after blinking a couple of times she saw that someone was now sitting at that desk.

"Hello?" she said quickly, trying not to panic. "Who are you?"

She waited, but the only reply was a faint murmur. After a moment she switched the phone's flashlight on again and tilted it up, yet the figure at the desk immediately faded away. Realizing that light seemed – for some reason – to make Edith Cole's ghost retreat, she lowered the phone and almost instantly heard the rustling sound once more.

Stumbling to her feet, she began to approach the desk.

"I want to help you," she said, trying to sound as calm as possible. "My name is Rebecca Pearson and I... I've been investigating things like... well, like you. Whatever you might actually turn out to be."

She hesitated.

"Do you... know that you're... not alive?"

Stopping in front of the desk, she was just about able to see that someone or something was sitting on the other side. She desperately wanted to hold the phone up and see properly, but she knew there was no point.

"I know your name is Edith Cole," she continued, "and I know you want to find out what happened to Meredith and Peter. I actually really want to find out the same thing, so if we could sort of... work together, we might have better luck. Do you think we can do that?"

She waited, but she heard no reply.

As her eyes adjusted a tad better to the darkness, and as just a slight hint of moonlight perhaps caught the window, she began to make out Edith Cole's features a little better. There was something instantly stark and authoritative about the woman, although Rebecca had to wonder how much of that was due to the fact that she'd been dead for many years. Surely, she figured, death had to take some of the wind out of a person's sails.

"I've searched everywhere I can think of," she told Edith. "There don't seem to be any hidden spaces where Meredith and Peter could have hidden. The windows were shut and you swore that they didn't walk past you on their way to the front door, so I really don't understand what's going on here."

She hesitated again, before forcing herself to lean a little closer.

"Is there something you're not telling me, Edith?" she continued. "Is there something you haven't told anyone? There must be, or -"

"Liar!" Edith snarled, suddenly looking up at her with dark, angry eyes. "You're just like all the rest! You think I must have had something to do with it! You think I hurt those poor children!"

"Then help me to help you... to prove them wrong," Rebecca said firmly. "Where are they, Edith? Where did Meredith and Peter go?"

"I don't know," Edith sobbed, her countenance changing in an instant as a large black spider began to crawl out from her mouth and tiny pinprick holes started to spread across one cheek. Tears were running from her eyes but already maggots were wriggling from rotten gaps in her face. "But they're close! I've felt it for as long as I've been here! They're so very close, so why can't I find them?"

CHAPTER TWENTY-THREE

"THERE'S NOTHING HERE," FATHER Rashford said as he stood in the doorway that led through to a backroom at the church. "I suppose one's senses can rather... conspire to trip one up in moments of heightened fear."

"If you mean you think you imagined it," Evelyn replied, peering past him but seeing nothing more than some old boxes filled with leftover flags and other items from the most recent St. George's Day celebrations, "then I ought to mention... I heard it too."

"And what did it sound like, Mrs. Ward?"

"Well, like... something getting up to something it shouldn't have."

"We have been plagued by mice since long before I arrived," he told her. "Sometimes I think I should employ the services of a parish cat."

"It didn't sound like mice to me," she murmured, before looking over her shoulder. "Where has that girl gotten to? Alicia? Don't be touching anything fragile!"

"This is all starting to feel like a wild goose chase," Father Rashford said, switching the light off and then stepping back before pulling the door shut. "Mrs. Ward, I'm terribly sorry that you've been dragged out here in the middle of the night at -"

"At my age?" she replied before he had a chance to finish that sentence.

"I wasn't going to say that."

"Then what *were* you going to say?"

"Perhaps we should call it a night," he continued diplomatically as he led her back through the church. "The children need their rest. Truly, I need some rest as well."

"Wait, wait," she spluttered, taking hold of his arm so that he could support her a little. "Don't tell my daughter this, but my legs aren't quite what they used to be. Or perhaps it's my hips. Or my knees."

They made slow progress past a set of shelves containing boxes of hymn books.

"Or all of me," she continued with a heavy sigh. "I'm sixty-seven years old, Father Rashford. I've always tried to look after myself, but time creeps up on us all."

"That it does, Mrs. Ward," he replied, nodding sagely. "That it does."

"Sometimes I even catch myself... forgetting the odd little thing," she added. "Nothing too important. I'm not too worried, I don't think it's anything serious. But I had a friend who forgot far more important things once. By the time she moved into the hospice, she wasn't even herself anymore."

Stopping, he turned to her.

"What did you just say?" he asked.

"I said that Gladys Ticklemole wasn't herself by the time she died," she continued, puzzled by his sudden interest. "Well, she *wasn't*! She even forgot her own husband. Can you believe that? Can you imagine what it must be like to forget the most important parts of your own life? We're all made of memories, Father Rashford. If we lose them, I honestly don't believe that we'd be the same person. Poor Gladys wasn't, not at the end. I went to see her once in the hospice, but she wasn't really herself. I suppose in some ways... the real Gladys had died a few years earlier, and all that was left was a shell walking around in her clothes. But she knew... she knew something was missing, even if she couldn't remember what it was."

"Like poor Father Pottinger, perhaps," he mused

"He wasn't well at the end, was he?" she pointed out.

"He most certainly was not," he continued, "and -"

Suddenly they both heard a loud cry coming from elsewhere in the church. They turned and looked past the altar, and a fraction of a second later Evelyn pulled away from the priest and hurried onward.

"That was my granddaughter!" she gasped breathlessly. "Alicia! Where are you?"

***

Crying out again as she was pulled deeper beneath the church's stone floor, Alicia turned and tried to find something – anything – she could grab onto and use to keep herself out of the darkness.

She could see the hole in the floor a little way above. Something had grabbed her and clamped its cold dead hand over her mouth, and then she'd been slowly pulled through the hole. Finally she'd managed to get her mouth free and cry out, but she could feel dead hands – gnarled like tree roots – pulling harder and harder, and she found herself now being forced backward into a tighter and tighter space.

"Help!" she cried out, even as she felt the scratching hands starting to tear her legs as she was pulled deeper and deeper still. "Someone help me!"

"Alicia?" she heard her grandmother shout

somewhere in the church. "Where are you?"

"I'm down here!" she gasped, twisting onto one side and trying to look down. "I'm -"

Before she could finish, she saw that two pairs of hands were clawing at her and dragging her into the depths. She instinctively tried to kick them away, only to slam her knees against the tightly compacted soil that lined the narrow space; she tried again, and after a few more attempts she was at least able to arrest her descent a little. Reaching out, she grabbed a partially buried set of bricks and managed to hold herself steady. The hands, meanwhile, were still grabbing at her but seemed somehow to have lost some of their strength.

"Alicia?"

Looking up, she was hugely relieved to see her grandmother peering down through the hole.

"Nana, help me!" she sobbed, only daring to reach up with one hand. "There's something down here!"

"What's going on?" Father Rashford asked, crouching down next to Evelyn. "What *is* this?"

"It looks like part of the floor gave way," Evelyn said, reaching through into the hole and trying to get to her granddaughter. "Alicia, can you take my hand?"

"I can't reach!" the girl sobbed.

"Let me try," Father Rashford replied, gently easing Evelyn out of the way and then leaning much further into the hole. "Alicia, try to take my hand and I'll pull you out. Please, you must hurry!"

Stretching and straining, Alicia felt the tips of the dead fingers digging into her legs but she forced herself to keep trying. Tears were streaming down her face and for a few seconds the entire enterprise felt utterly hopeless, but somehow she managed to extend her hand just a few more inches and finally she felt Father Rashford's fingers wrapping tight around her wrist.

"I'm going to pull you up!" he shouted.

"Hurry!"

"Please get her out of there," Evelyn stammered. "I don't understand what's happening!"

"On three!" Father Rashford said firmly. "Alicia... one... two..."

He hesitated for a fraction of a second.

"Three!"

With that, he pulled as hard as he could manage. Alicia, reaching out, managed to steady herself a little – and soon she was able to start scrambling up toward the hole in the floor again. She felt the dead hands slipping away from her legs, and finally she let out a set of heavy coughs as Father Rashford hauled her up and out onto the church's floor.

Coughing frantically, Alicia rolled onto her side before sitting up and looking back at the hole.

In that moment her grandmother pulled her tight for a hug.

"The floor just gave way," the girl stammered, trying not to panic. "Then they grabbed me!"

"Who grabbed you?" Father Rashford asked.

Looking deeper into the hole, Alicia was about to tell him about the hands when she suddenly realized that there was no need. She could *see* two pairs of hands still, but now she realized that they were much more skeletal than she'd previously realized and that they were attached to arms and perhaps even torsos. A moment later Father Rashford leaned past her and shone a flashlight down into the narrow space, and the beam of light picked out a pair of small pale skulls.

"Who are they?" Evelyn asked, squinting slightly as she tried to make out the full extent of the awful sight. "They're not very big. They almost look like..."

"Children," Father Rashford said as all the color drained from his face. "They're children. I think... I suppose we shall have to wait for formal identification, but I suppose they must be the two children who disappeared from here so long ago. I think these are the bodies of young Meredith Potter and Peter Swinson."

The three of them stared down at the bones

for a second as they tried to understand exactly what they were seeing.

"But... what are they doing in here?" Evelyn asked finally. "Why are they buried beneath the floor of the church? Father Rashford, I don't understand any part of this at all. Didn't they vanish from the school?"

Alicia was about to ask exactly what she meant, when she spotted movement out of the corner of one eye. Looking up, she was amazed to see Rose standing to one side of the altar, staring back at them all.

"Rose," she stammered. "Where have you been?"

"I've been watching you all," Rose replied calmly, glaring at them with a curiously detached expression on her face. After a moment, however, her expression changed and she allowed herself a faint sneer. "Why did you have to interfere in something that doesn't concern any of you?"

CHAPTER TWENTY-FOUR

STILL STANDING IN DARKNESS, Rebecca stared at the spot where she felt sure Edith Cole's ghost remained sitting at the desk. She wanted to say something that might help the dead woman, but in truth she could barely think straight. Finally, slowly, she switched the phone's flashlight on again and tilted the screen just a little, allowing herself to see a pair of pale dead hands resting on the desk's surface.

Convinced that she couldn't let too much light reach Edith's face – that to do so would mean chasing her away – Rebecca swallowed hard.

"If the children died here," she said finally, "then... then we must be able to find them."

She waited, but Edith said nothing.

"That's... that's just logic," Rebecca

continued. "At the very least, their bones must be here. Back in the 1950s, did the police use sniffer dogs? I would have thought that they'd take the entire place apart to find the bodies. I'm amazed the school is still standing at all."

Again she waited, but she could tell that she wasn't really getting through.

"I suppose things were different back then," she added, still trying to put everything together in her mind. "I'm sure they did their best, but obviously there was something they missed. Something important, something that was the key to it all, unless -"

"You," Edith Cole said suddenly, "are just like all the rest."

"What do you mean?"

"I mean that deep down," Edith continued, "in your heart of hearts, you believe that I had something to do with what happened to poor Meredith and Peter."

"I didn't say that."

"No, but you're thinking it," Edith said, before slowly getting to her feet. "There's no need to deny it. Do you have any idea what it was like after they vanished? People looked at me like I was... some sort of monster. Like I was hiding the truth."

"I'm sure no-one thought that."

"Of course they did!" Edith spat back at her.

"Every last one of them thought it! I would have moved away, but I had to look after my bedridden mother and... besides, why should I be chased away from my own home? And I didn't want to be seen to be running away from what had happened, I wanted to show them all that I was just as invested in the search. So I stubbornly stayed, convinced that eventually one day I'd find them, yet... find them, I did not. Nobody did."

"That doesn't mean that they're not here," Rebecca pointed out, struggling to keep from stepping back. "Miss Kemp -"

"What exactly do you think I did to them?" Edith sneered. "I'm sure everyone has had plenty of theories over the years. I'm sure the great and the good of Oxendon mulled over every single possibility. In fact, I imagine that there's only one possibility that they *didn't* consider, and that's the possibility that I was telling the truth and that I never did a single thing to harm anyone."

Sobbing now, she stepped closer and closer to Rebecca.

"But I got blamed for it!" she hissed angrily. "I got blamed for everything!"

"I'm sure that's not the case," Rebecca replied, before forcing herself to tilt the phone up, hoping to make the ghostly figure back away slightly. "I'm sure -"

In that instant she saw Edith's dead face,

with hollow eye sockets glaring back at her as the phone's light caught on exposed patches of the woman's skull. Thin hair hung down on either side of her face and scraps of flesh clung to the bone, and a moment later Edith tilted her head slightly to one side, causing the bones in her neck to scrape and grind against one another. For a fraction of a second Rebecca could only stare in horror, but finally her instincts took over and she couldn't help herself.

She ran.

Dropping her phone, she raced out into the corridor and almost fell as she hurried to the door. Grabbing the handle, she tried to pull it open, only to find that it wouldn't budge at all. She tried a couple more times, pulling harder and harder, until suddenly she froze as she realized that she could hear footsteps slowly emerging from the classroom. Turning, she saw nothing in the darkness but she felt absolutely certain that Edith Cole's ghost was on its way.

"I'm just trying to help you, Edith!" she shouted.

"Nobody can help me," the voice replied, edging ever closer. "Judgment was passed on my soul a long time ago, at least by the people of this fine village. If I ever leave this place, I am sure to face an even starker judgment, one that will have... lasting consequences."

"There has to be something everyone has missed," Rebecca stammered, still trying to get the door open. "Two children can't just vanish into thin air!"

"Yet they did," Edith said, and now she was even closer than before. "Perhaps I should just accept that it's all my fault," she added. "After all, when they came back to the school that evening, they were seeking my help. My support. My sanctuary. And I let them down."

"No!"

"Yes," Edith replied, "and the blame for that must ultimately remain with me. After all this time, I have finally understood *why* everyone judged me and why they were right to do so." She leaned closer, until her skeletal features were just about visible even in the darkness. "I should have saved them!"

***

"Rose, what are you talking about?" Alicia asked, struggling to hold back tears. "Rose, we found them. We found Meredith and Peter, they're buried right here. They've been under the church all along."

She waited, but Rose was merely staring back at her with a deeply unimpressed expression on her face.

"I don't know how they got here," Alicia continued, stepping forward until she reached the steps at the foot of the altar, "but... but something weird must have happened. The teacher must have been wrong all this time."

"We really ought to be getting home," Evelyn added. "Rose, do you knew where Rebecca might have gone?"

"Do you know what it's like," Rose replied darkly, "to struggle every day with the weight of evil in your soul?"

"What are you talking about?" Alicia asked. "Why -"

"Hush," Father Rashford said, placing a hand on her shoulder from behind. "I don't think we're talking to Rose right now," he continued, watching the figure next to the altar with a growing sense of suspicion. "It pains me to say this, but I rather think that we're talking to my predecessor. Somehow Father Pottinger is speaking *through* Rose."

"That's not possible," Evelyn whispered. "Why would you suggest such a thing?"

"Because it's true," Rose said, and now her voice sounded desperately harsh and scratched. "It's so much easier for me to communicate like this. I can... keep track of my thoughts a lot better. I can be far more articulate." She paused, before looking at the hole in the floor. "Every single day I struggled," she explained. "I pushed away the bad thoughts, I kept them hidden and I persuaded everyone that I was a good man."

A solitary tear began to run down one cheek.

"But sometimes there were temptations," she added, "and I always feared that one day I would break. I prayed and prayed and prayed for guidance, and I thought I had a chance, but deep down... I think I always knew that I would be bad once. Just one time in my life. And so it proved."

"What did you do to them?" Father Rashford asked.

"They came to the church one evening," Rose continued, "because... I'm not sure, exactly, but I think they'd finished at school and their parents weren't at home, and perhaps the front doors of their respective homes were locked. So they came to the church, and I made the mistake of saying that they could stay for a while."

"You took them in," Father Rashford pointed out. "That's not a bad thing."

"I shouldn't have allowed them to be anywhere near me," Father Pottinger said, still speaking through Rose's mouth. "I tried to hide away, but they came and found me. They seemed to sense that something was wrong, it was almost as if they were mocking or teasing me. You have no idea how hard I tried to stay good, how hard I prayed, but in truth I think nobody could have resisted that temptation. Eventually I... I reached out and put a hand on the young girl's shoulder, just an innocent hand but somehow I think she knew it meant more. And when I saw the fear and the realization in her eyes, I know I had revealed something of my true deep nature to her. I knew I couldn't let either of them tell anyone."

"What did you do to them?" Evelyn asked, pulling Alicia close. "What did you do to those poor children?"

"Not what I wanted to do," the voice snarled, "but they were scared and I panicked. The church's floor was being relaid, there was just a small portion left to be completed, but there were lots of spare bricks around. It was as if temptation had been placed before me, and for once in my miserable life... I weakened."

"And what did you do then?" Father Rashford asked, and now his voice was thick with tension. "Father Pottinger... *why* did you kill Meredith and Peter?"

CHAPTER TWENTY-FIVE

1956...

STANDING IN THE CHURCH, in almost the exact spot where decades later he would possess the body of Rose Radcliffe, Father Pottinger stared down at the lifeless corpses of Meredith Swinson and Peter Potter.

Blood was splattered on the sides of their heads, and more blood was caked on the stone brick in the priest's right hand.

"I... I'm so sorry," he stammered finally, breaking a silence that had lasted for several minutes since the final agonized cries had rung out. "I didn't mean... I just..."

His voice trailed off for a few seconds.

"I panicked," he added as tears began to run from his eyes. "No, wait... *you* panicked. I don't know what you thought I was going to do, but I only touched your shoulder. That's all. What is the world coming to if a man can't..."

Again he fell silent, before setting the bloodied brick on the altar and then holding his trembling hand up so that he could see it better.

"But you sensed something, didn't you?" he whispered. "You sensed that there was something darker in my soul, something I have always struggled to contain. Something that has been within me since I was but a child myself. Yet is it fair that I should pay the ultimate price for that? If a man is good for almost every moment of his life and then bad for just a minute or two, should he be condemned? I can push my desires back down, I can ignore them again. And I can be a good man, I can be the priest this parish needs. Why should others suffer because of *my* mistake?"

He turned his hand around.

"They need me," he purred. "All of the people here... they wouldn't be able to get along without me."

He watched for a moment as his hand continued to shake, and then he looked once more at the two dead children. Then, slowly, he looked past them and saw a patch on the floor that had not yet been covered over by the builders. In that moment, he felt as if the solution to his problem was so simple and so miraculously evident that it was almost as if it had been offered to him by a divine hand, as if some other force was nudging him and telling him that he could go on.

"I shall spend the rest of my life making up for this," he muttered, stepping around the children and then grabbing Meredith's hands. He hauled her to the hole in the floor and pushed her through, and to his amazement he saw that she slithered down out of sight. "This truly *is* a miracle," he added. "They won't even end up in the crypt. They'll just be... gone. Forever."

He quickly grabbed Peter and pushed him down into the same space, and he realized that even the builders would have no reason to peer down there too deeply. Upon their return they would merely finish the floor and seal it all up, and then the children would be out of sight for the rest of time. Certainly questions would be asked in the village, but he wasn't aware that anyone had seen them entering the church; and even if they had, nobody would ever dare to question the actions of a man in his position.

Stepping back, he sat on one of the pews.

He was still shaking, but he felt more and more certain that everything was going to be alright.

"I shall pray for your souls," he whispered, staring at the hole. "Every day, for the rest of my life, I shall pray for your souls and the souls of all those whose lives were touched by your presence. And I promise, with all my heart, that I shall never again commit an act of such evil. For the rest of my days I shall once again bring nothing but kindness and understanding to this world."

***

"There she is," a woman muttered, keeping her voice low – but not so low that she couldn't be heard across the street. "I can't believe the gall of that wretch. Does she truly believe that the rest of us want to see her hideous face ever again?"

Trying to ignore yet more comments, Edith Cole continued to make her way along the village street. She rarely ventured out of the house these days, often saving up her errands so that they could all be completed in one or two trips. On those rare occasions when she had to go out, however, she always prepared herself for the unkind comments that she would undoubtedly hear from others.

Six   months   had   passed   since   the

disappearances of Meredith Potter and Peter Swinson, and deep down Edith knew full well that there was no chance now that they might ever be found alive.

Ahead, two more women were already sneering at her as she made her way closer, yet she had no choice. After all, she had to fetch some items for her mother.

"Good morning," she said softly, still determined to be polite.

The women stared at her as she passed but offered no greeting in return.

And then, just as she was about to go into the shop, Edith flinched as she felt a cold glob of spit hitting the back of her neck hard. She froze for a moment, telling herself that she had to be wrong, and then she reached up and wiped the spit away. Looking at the glistening, slimy substance on her fingers, she felt a shiver run through her bones before slowly turning to look at the women.

She had no idea which of them had spat on her, but they were both glaring with expressions of undisguised disgust.

"I am sorry to excite such venom in your breasts," she stammered, feeling as if she finally had to defend herself once more. Close to tears now, she was nevertheless determined to keep from showing too much emotion. "I can only reiterate that -"

"Save your lies," one of the women sneered. "The school most likely won't ever open its doors again. You won't even have a job. Are you really going to stick around when you know how much you're hated here?"

"I'm going to visit the police station again next week," Edith told them. "I... I have been thinking, and perhaps there are some other possibilities that were overlooked."

"And what might those be?" the other woman asked.

"They're just... theories right now," Edith explained, "but it's possible that something might come of them. I mean, it's worth a try, is it not?"

"Ladies," Father Pottinger said, stepping out from the shop and clearly recognizing the difficulty of the situation. "It's such a nice morning. I trust that all is well?"

"All *was* well," one of the women said, as she and her companion turned and walked away, "until that awful sight showed up."

Edith watched them heading off along the street. Now that they were gone, she was no longer able to hide the tears that even now were welling in her eyes.

"It's sunny," Father Pottinger pointed out, sounding a little uncomfortable now. "A nice day. You should enjoy it, Miss Cole."

With that, he began to walk past her.

"Father?" she said, turning to him. "Do you think that I'm doing the right thing? By staying here, I mean. Mother needs me, but one day when she is gone, should I remain and still try to find Meredith and Peter, or should I leave so that people here no longer have to see my face?"

"I really don't know what is best," he replied awkwardly. "That decision is for you, and you alone."

"But what would you do?"

"I... would not be in such a position in the first place," he told her. "I would simply not allow it."

"Of course," she said softly, lowering her gaze as she felt his judging eyes staring into her soul. "Father, I'm sorry, I only wondered. The truth is, I still don't know how to deal with this situation. The police are satisfied that I know nothing more about poor Meredith and Peter, yet it seems that everyone else in the village blames me. As they probably should." She looked up at him again. "But *you* know that I am innocent, do you not? Of all people, you must see that I am only trying to do the right thing."

"I must get going," he told her, before turning and hurrying along the street.

"Will you not even pray for me?" she called after him, but his silence was her only reply. "Will no-one else pray for me?" she asked quietly. "Even my own mother... I know she doubts me. Everyone doubts me."

Glancing around, she saw several more people in the street – and all of them were eyeing her with varying degrees of suspicion. Finally, feeling as if their attention might be about to cause her to combust, she turned and hurried away while telling herself that she could return and get things from the shop on another day. In that moment, she simply wanted to hide away forever.

CHAPTER TWENTY-SIX

Many years later...

"I HAVE BROUGHT YOU some nettle tea," Father Rashford said, stopping in the doorway for a moment and looking over at the pale and emaciated man in the bed. "I... I know that it is your favorite."

He waited for Father Pottinger to reply, yet in truth he knew that the elderly man was unlikely to say much at all. For a few days now, since taking to his bed, Father Pottinger had seemed more wrapped up in his own thoughts than ever before, as if in his final moments he was barely aware of the rest of the world at all.

Father Rashford knew a dying man when he saw one.

"Well, it's already cooling," Father Rashford

continued, taking the cup over and setting it on the nightstand. "I shan't disturb you too much. It's late, so if there's nothing else that you require, I shall retire for the night."

He turned to leave the room.

"Also, if any -"

"Are they here?" Father Pottinger gasped, suddenly reaching out and grabbing him by the arm.

"Who?" Father Rashford asked, shocked by the forcefulness of the man's grip. "Who are you talking about?"

"Where is the Cole woman? What has become of her?"

"The Cole woman?"

Father Rashford hesitated for a moment as he tried to make sense of his predecessor's rambling words. He was more than accustomed to Father Pottinger rambling and referring to fragments of the past, but this time the man's words seemed a little more pointed and focused.

"Do you mean... Edith Cole? The former schoolteacher?"

"Bring her to me!"

"I can't possibly do that, Father Pottinger. Edith Cole died some years ago."

"She did?"

"I believe you officiated at her funeral. I have heard it remarked that the occasion was rather sparsely attended. Indeed, from what I have been told, the only attendees besides yourself were the two gentlemen who used to dig and fill graves back in those days. I have seen her grave myself, unfortunately it has deteriorated rather rapidly. I keep meaning to do something to fix it but, well, I'm not sure where to start."

"I..."

Father Pottinger seemed momentarily shocked by this news, before slowly sinking back down against his pillow.

"Of course," he murmured. "Mmm. Yes, of course."

"Why would you want to speak to Miss Cole now?" Father Rashford asked cautiously. "Were you particularly close to her?"

"I don't know," Father Pottinger murmured. "I don't remember. For a moment I was seized by the most awful sense that I should talk to the woman, but now I cannot recollect why I felt that way."

"You should get some rest," Father Rashford said, surprised by the man's brief insistence – but quickly telling himself that there was no reason to be unduly concerned. "I must admit, I never fully understood the sheer hatred that Miss Cole seems to have received in Oxendon. People can be so cruel when they believe they are in the right. I can only hope that her soul is now at rest."

"What?" Father Pottinger stammered.

"What are you talking about?"

"Try to sleep," Father Rashford said, slipping free from his grip and heading to the door. "I'm sure you'll feel better in the morning."

Yet the following morning, when he went back into the room to rouse Father Pottinger for another day, Father Rashford instead found that the older man was stiff and dead in his bed, and quite cold to the touch. He sat with the corpse for a few minutes while praying for his soul, and then he left the room in order to make the necessary arrangements. And from that day, he gave scarcely any thought to the man's final rambling request to see the long dead Miss Edith Cole.

***

Ten years later...

"You forgot, didn't you?" Father Rashford said, still staring at Rose as he sensed Father Pottinger's soul glaring back at him from the child's eyes. "You weren't lying about that. By the end of your life, the dementia had robbed you of so many memories, but a kind of... echo persisted, did it not? An echo of the one day in your life when you were truly a bad person."

"I remember it all now," she replied, channeling the dead priest's words with apparent ease. "If only they hadn't panicked so much, everything would have been alright."

"They probably didn't panic at all," Father Rashford continued. "They were so young. They were playing. They probably didn't even understand that they were in danger. At least, not until it was too late.."

"I always struggled with bad thoughts," Rose snarled. "The most terrible ideas and impulses would intrude into my mind, almost compelling me to take them seriously. And when they finally came bursting out of me, just for a minute or two, they did more damage to my life than I ever believed possible. Since that day I have lived with the guilt, even if over time I began to forget what the guilt was even *for*. And then after I died, everything became clear again once I found myself back here in the church, doomed to linger near the scene of my awful crime."

"Did he really kill them?" Alicia whispered, looking up at her grandmother. "I don't understand why."

"I think I can guess," Evelyn replied through gritted teeth, keeping her eyes fixed on Rose. "He wouldn't be the first and he won't be the last."

"But -"

"You're too young," Evelyn added. "To understand, I mean. To be told of such things."

"But why is he in Rose's body?" Alicia continued, trying to ignore the fact that she hated being told she was too young to understand anything. "How can we get him out?"

"I don't know," Evelyn said, shaking her head.

"I only did one thing wrong," Rose went on. "One tiny, little thing that was over in a matter of minutes. Seconds, really. For the rest of my life, both before and after, I made sure that I was a good person. Why should I pay for a moment of weakness?"

"Because it wasn't just one moment," Father Rashford replied. "Not if I understand correctly.. You knew what had happened to those children, yet you allowed Miss Cole to carry the burden of suspicion for the rest of her life. You allowed her to be the most hated woman in Oxendon until she went to her grave."

"I -"

"It's your fault that nobody went to her funeral," he added. "It's your fault that even now she haunts the school building. You let that woman be tortured by lies and rumors, when you could so easily have stopped it all."

"Not easily!" Rose barked. "It could never have been easy!"

"You should have confessed," Father Rashford said firmly. "You should not have hidden your guilt and allowed its burden to fall upon the shoulders of another. If you had confessed, Miss Cole would have been spared and you might in time have gained forgiveness from the Lord."

"It's not my fault that people reacted the way they did," Rose snarled. "I didn't *make* them turn on the teacher."

"And now you occupy the body of young Rose," Father Rashford pointed out, taking a step forward. "Is *that* right?"

"I did not choose this," she replied, and for the first time her voice sounded more than a little unsteady. "I was almost... drawn to take possession of her. She is different to all the rest of you, you know. There is something about her that is much more receptive to the undead. It is as if she, and she alone, can always sense our fears and our torment."

"That is as may be," Father Rashford said firmly, "but I command you to leave her body at once. Do you understand, Father Pottinger? I will not stand by and let you hurt anyone else! The two sets of bones beneath the church are going to be lifted out and given a proper burial. The truth will be revealed and Miss Cole, even in retrospect, will be cleared of all wrongdoing."

"So that my name is dragged through the mud?"

"So that things are put back to how they should be," Father Rashford continued, betraying a hint of anger. "You must realize that this is the right thing to do. Is there not a shred of decency left in you? The Father Pottinger I knew *was* a good man, I could see that. I did not know about his past, but I knew that the man before me – despite the loss of much of his mind – was a decent and honorable human being. He would have done the right thing, had he remembered the truth of his past actions."

"How easily you separate us," Rose sneered. "We are – we were – the same man."

"Then prove it!" Father Rashford shouted. "Find him in you now and -"

Before he could finish, Rose raised a hand and – without touching him – sent him flying back through the air until he crashed down against several pews.

"Run!" Evelyn shouted, turning to push Alicia toward the door. "Get out of -"

In that instant she too was sent crashing along the aisle. As Alicia ducked down out of sight between one row of pews, she heard her grandmother slam into the ground, and she turned to see that she had already lost consciousness.

"Poor judgmental Father Rashford," Rose purred, stepping down from the altar and making her way slowly toward the priest as he tried to get to his feet. "Do you really think I'll allow my name to be besmirched after all these years? The parents of those two ratty children are long gone now. Why should I suffer just so that you and others like you can feel superior?"

CHAPTER TWENTY-SEVEN

"YOU COULDN'T SAVE THEM," Rebecca stammered, staring into the dead eyes of Edith Cole and – at the same time – pulling back harder against the school's front door. "You couldn't save them because you're not the one who did anything to them in the first place. Are you really going to allow this guilt to twist your soul and turn you into a monster?"

She waited, hoping desperately that she might have managed to get through to her, yet all she saw in return was a kind of simmering anger that seemed poised to boil over at any moment.

"I don't know exactly when you died," she continued, "but if you've been trapped here ever since, haunting this school and trying to find the children, festering in a sense of shame..."

Her voice trailed off for a few more seconds.

"I understand," she added finally, "but you have to realize that it wasn't your fault. Whatever happened to those two children, you're not responsible. It doesn't matter what other people in the village claimed. The school was supposed to be closed, you did everything you could. I don't know where they went, or how they got out of the classroom without being seen, or why their bodies have never been found but... you can't let people blame you."

"I should have taken care of them," Edith said softly, withdrawing a little deeper into the shadows. "I should have done better."

"And now you're scared to move on," Rebecca said. "Is that it? Forgive me, Edith, I'm still kind of new to understanding all of this. Are you... trying to avoid moving to whatever comes next? Do you *know* what comes next?"

"I feel it waiting for me."

"What?" Rebecca asked. "What do you feel waiting?"

"Eternity. Judgment."

"You make it sounds almost... religious."

"There's a place beyond this world," Edith whispered. "I haven't seen it yet, because once I see it there'll be no coming back. For now I wait here endlessly, desperate to find the children so that I can perhaps guide them. I know that I shall face eternal damnation, but might I not at least save poor Meredith and Peter? I couldn't help them in life, but perhaps I might yet help them in death."

"That seems like a tall order," Rebecca pointed out.

"I should have known that you'd never understand," Edith sneered. "You're just like all the rest, aren't you? You think you're better than me!"

"No!" Rebecca gasped, trying the door's handle again but still finding that it wouldn't budge. "Edith, listen to me, I -"

"You look at me the same way they always used to look at me," she continued. "I haven't dared to leave this school in years, not since I drew my final breath out there in the world. And I never *will* leave it, either. I won't put one foot beyond the threshold until I have found those two precious children. As for you, I can only despise you for judging me like all the others."

"No, I -"

"And I shall make you pay for that," Edith added, pulling back further – until she was out of sight entirely. "I shall make you pay in the only currency I have left. Fear. And the price will be your life."

"Wait," Rebecca replied, pulling back against the door once more, "what -"

Suddenly Edith screamed and lunged at her.

Pulling back harder, Rebecca waited for the ghostly woman to slam into her, but at the very last second the door suddenly buckled behind her and swung open. Startled, she tumbled out and landed hard on the step just as the ghostly form of Edith Cole rushed over her and faded away into the cold night air outside the school building.

"Mum?"

Turning, Rebecca was shocked to see that Alicia was the one who'd opened the door.

"I came looking for you," the girl stammered, "and I heard your voice coming from in here. Mum, something's really wrong in the church. It's Rose, I think... I think a ghost has taken over Rose's body..."

***

Racing into the church, Rebecca stopped as soon as she heard a faint choking sound. She listened for a moment before hurrying past the empty rows of pews, and finally she spotted Father Rashford on the ground with Rose straddling him and clutching his throat.

"Leave him alone!" Rebecca yelled, rushing over and pulling Rose away. "What are you doing?"

Nearby, Evelyn was still struggling to get to her feet.

"It's not Rose!" Alicia said firmly, her voice

filling with fear as she held back. "Mum, be careful, she -"

In that moment Rose lunged at Rebecca, slamming her fists into her chest and knocking her back.

"Rose, what are you doing?" Rebecca stammered, trying to push her away. "Rose, stop that! You're hurting me!"

"It's the old priest!" Alicia sobbed as she saw Father Rashford sitting up and gasping for air. "Mum, the old priest has taken control of Rose!"

"That's impossible!" Rebecca replied, grabbing Rose's arms and trying to hold her still. "Rose, listen to me, you have to stop this immediately!"

Having seen what was happening, Father Rashford stumbled over and grabbed Rose's ankles, and then together he and Rebecca lifted her away.

"Let go of me!" the girl screamed, struggling furiously. "You can't let the world know what I did!"

"What's she talking about?" Rebecca yelled.

"Father Pottinger killed the two children," Father Rashford said breathlessly, still just about managing to keep hold of Rose's ankles. "He buried them in here. It seems that he struggled all his life with certain... dark thoughts, and on one day back in 1956 he allowed those feelings out for a moment or two. The results were catastrophic."

"But how's he possessing Rose?" Rebecca asked.

"I have no idea," he told her. "He said something about being drawn to her."

Horrified as she watched the adults struggling to subdue Rose, Alicia stepped back as she tried to work out how she might be able to help. She looked around, and after a moment she spotted a figure outside, beyond the church's open door. She stared for a few seconds, not quite understanding what she was seeing, before finally realizing that the woman was wearing an old-fashioned dress and that she seemed to be the ghostly form of Edith Cole. In that moment, as she heard Rose still yelling, she was suddenly struck by a moment of realization.

"No-one can know!" Rose snarled. "You have to stop them finding out!"

Hurrying past the first pews, Alicia immediately dropped down and clambered back into the hole. She struggled slightly to slither down, but after a few seconds she managed to reach the bones of the children. Gathering as many of those bones up as possible, and making sure to get both the skulls, she then hauled herself back up with great difficulty until finally she managed to climb over the edge. Still clutching the bones, she turned and saw that Rose had spotted her; filled with rage and fury, Rose screamed and threw both Rebecca and Father Rashford aside before getting up and racing forward.

Realizing that this might be her last chance, Alicia turned and ran along the aisle, hurrying toward the door. She could still see the ghost of Edith Cole outside, but she could also hear Rose's breathless gasps getting closer and closer behind her. And then, just as she thought she was about to be caught, she stumbled through the open doorway and dropped to her knees, spilling the bones out onto the grass.

"Stop!" Rose screamed, grabbing her from behind and pulling her back. "You can't move them!"

Slipping free, Alicia pushed her aside and looked up just in time to see Edith staring at the bones.

"They were never in the school," she explained breathlessly, hoping to get through to the ghostly teacher. "All this time they were buried under the church, they've been there since they disappeared. I don't know how they got there from the school, but it's not your fault that they died. It was the priest who was here at the time, he did something to them, I think he... I think he murdered them. I don't know the details, but what matters is that it wasn't your fault! Everyone was wrong about you! You didn't do anything bad!"

Edith stared at the bones for a moment

longer before looking directly at Alicia. And then, slowly, she looked back down and saw two small hands reaching out toward her. She turned, and finally she found herself flanked by the ghostly figures of Meredith Potter and Peter Swinson. With tears in her eyes, Edith hesitated for a few more seconds before turning and allowing the children to lead her away across the cemetery, and after a moment all three of them faded away into the night air.

"She found them," Alicia stammered, shivering slightly in the cold night air despite her grandfather's heavy coat. "She finally found them and I think... I think now she can rest in peace."

CHAPTER TWENTY-EIGHT

"NO, I'M REALLY QUITE alright," Father Rashford said as he sat on one of the pews, using a handkerchief to dab at a wound on his head. "Please don't fuss. What about your mother?"

"My legs are hurting," Evelyn said from one of the other pews. "That's normal, though. At my age, anyway."

Rebecca turned to her.

"Slightly," Evelyn added. "It's not a big deal. All things considered, I'm still rather spry."

"I still think we should get you both to the hospital," Rebecca told them, figuring that this wasn't the moment to get into another argument about mobility. "Just to get you checked over."

"And what would we tell them?" Father Rashford asked. "That we were attacked by a ghost?

They'd be scanning our brains in no time."

"No-one's scanning *my* brain," Evelyn said firmly. "I'm not letting them bombard me with weird rays. There's nothing wrong with me that a good night's sleep won't fix. And perhaps a glass of brandy before I turn in."

"It'll soon be breakfast time," Rebecca pointed out.

"I know. That's what made me think of brandy."

Realizing that there *really* was no point arguing with her mother, Rebecca turned and made her way over to the spot where Alicia was sitting with Rose. Ever since the ghostly figures of Edith and the children had vanished, Rose had fallen entirely silent and she now seemed to be lost in her own thoughts. As much as she didn't want to fuss, Rebecca couldn't help but worry that the girl was suffering some side effects from her time hosting the ghost of Father Pottinger.

"How are we doing here?" she asked finally.

"I've got a headache," Rose said cautiously.

"No kidding."

"I think she's going to be okay," Alicia said confidently, looking up at her mother. "I think he left her now."

"To go where?" Father Rashford called over to them.

"He was haunting the church because he

didn't want anyone to find the bones," Rebecca explained. "At least, that's my working theory. Now that the secret is out, he probably doesn't see any reason to linger. He knows that everyone will find out about his past, and that there's literally nothing more that he can do to change things. I imagine that must have removed much of the motivation for him to cling to this world."

"So he's really gone?" Alicia asked.

"It seems that way."

"But..."

She paused before turning to Rose again.

"What if he comes back?" she added. "What if he's hiding in her head? What if, now he has a connection, he can stay in her and still control her?"

"He can't," Rose said softly, finally looking up first at Alicia and then at Rebecca. "He's gone."

"Are you sure?" Rebecca asked.

Rose nodded.

"I'm so sorry you went through this," Rebecca continued. "Rose, if I'd had any idea how dangerous this was going to be, I never would have brought either of you."

"It's not that I invited him in, exactly," she replied, "it's more that when I sensed his ghost, I couldn't help myself. I knew that I needed to get into his thoughts and that the only way to do that was for us to share the same body for a few minutes. He was so angry, at himself and at everyone else, but he genuinely believed that he shouldn't be judged for what he'd done to those children. He thought that his lifetime of good work should outweigh a moment of weakness."

"I'm not sure that it works that way," Rebecca told her. "I'm also fairly sure that, even if there *is* some kind of judgment at the end of everything, it's not our place to try to see it coming. Best to leave that to..."

She fell silent for a few seconds.

"To who?" Alicia asked.

"I really don't know," Rebecca admitted, and now she seemed more than a little uncomfortable. "Father Pottinger and Miss Cole certainly both seemed convinced that staying here allowed them to hide from something else. I must admit, part of me wishes they'd stayed around for a little while longer so that I could have picked their brains. There's obviously so much still going on that none of us can possibly understand."

"I for one would like to leave it that way," Father Rashford suggested. "I'm really not sure that it's a good idea for us to go poking around in things that are beyond this world. After all, they're beyond for a reason."

"I'm a scientist first and foremost," Rebecca reminded him, albeit with a hint of doubt in her voice. "It's my job to poke around in things that I don't understand. And one day I'm going to find a

THE HAUNTING OF OXENDON SCHOOL

way to understand exactly what went on here tonight."

* * *

The following morning, sitting in the kitchen of her grandmother's cottage, Alicia idly stirred her bowl of cereal as she replayed the previous night's events over and over again.

A moment later, hearing footsteps approaching the doorway, she turned just in time to see Rose entering the room.

"Hey," Rose said awkwardly.

"Hey," Alicia replied.

Rose hesitated for a few seconds before pouring herself a glass of nettle juice and taking a seat.

"How are you feeling?" Alicia asked.

"I'm okay," Rose replied, before thinking for a moment. "I think."

They sat in silence as they each tried to come up with a way to make the situation less strange.

"I'm sorry," Rose added finally.

"For what?"

"For being weird."

"You're not -"

Before she could finish that sentence, Alicia realized that there was probably no point lying.

"It's okay," she said softly. "What... what was it like being possessed by a ghost?"

Rose shrugged.

"That's okay," Alicia continued. "If you don't want to talk about it, then -"

"It's not that I don't want to talk about it," Rose replied. "I just don't know how to describe it. It's like I could tell that there were ghosts nearby, and then one of them was sort of... pulled into me. I was still me, but I could feel his anger and I could read his thoughts." She thought for a moment longer. "Then at the end, after the bones went outside, I felt him giving up. It was like he suddenly knew that there was no point staying, and he was really scared but he allowed himself to go somewhere else."

"Where?"

"I don't know."

"I don't think my mum and dad know, either," Alicia pointed out. "I think that's one of the things they want to find out with their experiments."

"I don't know if they should," Rose said cautiously.

"What do you mean?"

"When the old priest was leaving my body, he was really scared. He was more scared than anyone I've ever heard of before. And just as he went away, I think I sort of... sensed a bit of where he was going. It didn't seem very nice."

"What was wrong with it?"

"It just seemed... different. And I don't think he was going to have a very nice time there."

"I don't think he was a very nice man," Alicia pointed out.

"I suppose not," Rose admitted. "I think he was guarding those bones because he wanted to keep *pretending* that he was nice, though. Or maybe he was nice but part of him wasn't. I don't know. People are confusing sometimes, but overall... I'm really glad that he's gone."

"It was pretty strange when you were possessed," Alicia told her.

"Did my voice sound different?"

"No, it was more your eyes. They didn't seem like they were really *your* eyes, if that makes sense. I could sort of tell that someone else was looking out through them." She paused again, wondering whether she should dare to ask the question that was really bothering her. "Do you think it'll happen again? Being possessed, I mean. Do you think that every time you go near a ghost, they'll be able to take you over like that?"

"I don't know."

"Aren't you scared?"

Although she thought about that question for a few seconds, Rose quickly realized that she really wasn't sure of the answer. She knew she definitely *should* be scared, and she definitely didn't like the way the ghostly priest had entered her body and had pushed her soul aside, but at the same time she also found the entire situation fascinating. As much as she didn't really want to admit the fact, part of her needed to understand what had happened and – perhaps more importantly – to understand exactly where the ghosts had all gone. After all, she was fairly sure that Father Pottinger and the others were no longer haunting the village.

"Not yet," she admitted finally. "I might be one day, but I'm not scared at the moment."

"That's really brave."

"It's not brave," Rose replied. "I just want to know, that's all. It's like your mum said. How can anyone not want to know if there's a whole other world out there?"

CHAPTER TWENTY-NINE

STANDING IN THE GARDEN, Rebecca continued to watch through the window as Alicia and Rose talked at the kitchen table. A moment later, hearing footsteps on the path, she turned to see her mother making her way over with a basket of flowers in one hand.

"Done!" Evelyn announced triumphantly. "All those dead heads are finally gone! The borders look beautiful and my soup prep can begin."

"About the stair rail system -"

"Are you still banging on about that?" Evelyn asked with a sigh. "I told you, I don't need help getting up the stairs. That sort of thing is for old people."

"Mum -"

"Did you ever work out what really

happened to those children?" Evelyn continued, pointedly interrupting her daughter. "I must admit, I wasn't paying attention to all of it, but my understanding was that you were wondering how the children managed to get out of the school without being seen. I know they were found in the church, but do you think they simply crept out when their teacher wasn't looking and then... went to their doom?"

"That's possible," Rebecca said, picking her words with care, "but actually I've come up with another theory that I think makes much more sense."

"Oh, another of your *theories*," Evelyn replied, rolling her eyes. "Go on, then. Entertain me with it all."

"I went and took another look at the school building this morning," Rebecca continued. "Don't worry, I'm pretty sure that there are no ghosts there. Not now. In fact, the place felt much lighter and... more free, somehow. But as I was looking around and trying to find any kind of hidden panel, I realized that Edith Cole must have been *really* sure that the children didn't leave. After all, she staked her entire reputation on that fact and she never wavered from the conviction. If there had been any doubt in her mind at all, don't you think she would have seized it?"

"So what do you think really happened?"

"I think the children were far more fond of their teacher than any of us realized," Rebecca explained. "And I don't think they vanished from the classroom at all. At least, not in the way that everyone has been thinking."

***

1956...

"I'm afraid I don't have anything for you to do," Edith explained as she stopped in the classroom and watched the two children heading to a couple of desks. "This is all very irregular, but you'll simply have to sit there until I'm done. And then, if your parents still aren't home... I have to ask, where are they? Peter, your father always finishes at the mill in the early afternoon. Where are he and your mother?"

"We think they're out," Meredith said before Peter could answer for himself.

"And what about *your* parents?" Edith continued.

"They must be out too, I suppose," Meredith replied. "We're sorry, Miss Cole, we don't want you to be angry with us. If you want us to leave, we can."

"Heavens, no," Edith muttered. "Just sit down and... and find some way to amuse yourselves. In fact, in a minute or two I might have a job that you can do. Some of the older books need arranging. Do you think you'd like to do that?"

"We would," Meredith said, "but -"

"Let me fetch them," Edith added, turning and hurrying out of the room. "Just one moment!" she called back to the children. "In fact, do you want to come and give me a hand? Come along, children, and fetch some of the books so that you can sort them. Remember, the Devil makes work for idle hands!"

Left sitting alone in the classroom, Meredith and Peter stared at the open doorway for a moment before slowly turning to each other. At first neither of them said anything; neither of them could quite understand what had happened, and the glance they shared was one of fear. Time seemed almost to slow down as they sat patiently, but finally it was Meredith who looked away and instead touched the desk.

"It feels... different," she said softly.

"What do you mean?" Peter whispered.

"It just feels different," she continued. "Like... I shouldn't be touching it. I don't know, I can't explain, but it just feels wrong."

"You should ask Miss Cole," he replied.

"I don't think she'll know."

"She knows everything," he pointed out, with just a hint of desperation in his voice. "She's the best teacher ever. I always liked her much more than anyone else, she even helped me when I was having trouble with my times tables. It was thanks to her that my dad stopped getting angry at me all the time and calling me stupid. She's really nice and..."

His voice trailed off now as he remembered encountering Father Pottinger in the church.

"Why did he hurt us?" he asked after a few more seconds.

"I don't know."

"I thought he was nice," he added. "Everyone always says that Father Pottinger's a good person, so why did he..."

He held his hands up and stared at them.

"I don't quite remember what he did," he murmured. "I know it hurt, and I know I was scared and... and I was bleeding. I saw you were bleeding too. He was holding that candlestick holder and there was blood dripping from one end. And then everything got confused, and suddenly we were standing at the other end of the church watching as..."

Although he recalled the sight of Father Pottinger shoving two small bodies down through a hole in the floor, he wasn't quite able to bring himself to accept the truth.

"We're down there now," Meredith said quietly, almost too quietly to be heard.

"But how *can* we be?" he asked, trying not to panic. "We're here! We're both right here in the classroom!"

"We came here because it's the only place we can feel safe," she told him as she heard the teacher's voice in the distance, "but... if we stay, Miss Cole is going to realize what happened. I don't think we should let that happen. I think we should wait outside, maybe near the church, and hope that someone finds us down there."

"But what -"

"It's the only way, Peter," she added.

"But I'm scared," he told her.

"So am I."

She reached over and took hold of her hand.

"It'll be okay," she continued. "We'll keep each other company while we wait. I don't know whether we should try to go home, either. I don't want to scare anyone. I think we should try to stay out of the way and not let people see us, and just hope that eventually someone finds us in the church. It shouldn't take too long, should it? Father Pottinger might confess, or someone will look in the hole or... I don't know, but somehow it's all going to be alright. We just have to be patient."

"Can't we go home just one time?" he asked. "I want to see my mum and dad."

"They'd be too scared," she insisted. "We're..."

She hesitated, as if she wasn't quite sure that she could even get the words out.

"We're ghosts now, Peter," she added finally, as her voice became tense with fear. "That's just the truth and we can't change it. I don't know about you, but I don't want to be the scary sort of ghost either. I just want to be buried properly, like everyone else. And you never know, eventually we might be able to help someone to find us."

"How?"

"I really don't know," she added, "but... we have to try."

Hearing Miss Cole's voice again, she squeezed Peter's hand a little tighter.

"And let's start by not scaring her," she said softly. "I really like her, and I know you do too. Let's make sure that she doesn't realize what we are now."

They stared at each other for a moment, and then they both faded from view just as footsteps hurried toward the doorway.

"You really must buck up your ideas a little," Miss Cole told them as she entered. "It does nobody any good if you just -"

Stopping suddenly, she saw that all the desks were now bare and unattended, and that there was absolutely no sign of either Meredith or Peter.

"Children?" she said again, wondering where they could possibly have gone.

Stepping forward, she heard a cracking sound and felt a floorboard creaking beneath her feet.

"You can't have gone out through the front door," she said under her breath. "I would have seen you."

She took another step forward, and another floorboard gently shifted under the pressure.

"Children?" she called out for a third time. "I'm really too busy and too tired for any foolishness, so will you please make yourselves known at once? Children, where are you?"

CHAPTER THIRTY

Many years later...

"YOU REALLY THINK THAT'S what happened?"
Jonathan said as he stood in the kitchen at the
Pearsons' home, stirring a pan of soup. "You think
they were dead by the time they showed up at the
school and *that's* why they were able to disappear
without anyone noticing?"

"It makes sense," Rebecca pointed out.

He turned to her.

"It does if you just accept the idea that
ghosts might behave like that," she continued,
realizing that she needed to emphasize her point a
little more. "They probably went back to the school
because it felt like a safe place, and because they
thought Edith Cole would protect them. I have no

idea what it must feel like to suddenly be dead, but I imagine that at least in some cases these souls understand that something has changed."

"Well, it's not the craziest idea I've ever heard," he admitted. "Close, but... not quite."

"There's still so much we don't know about these things," she said with a sigh. "I feel like so far we've just been picking at the edges. I got an email from Father Rashford earlier, he thinks Father Pottinger's ghost is no longer haunting the church and he's arranging for the bodies of the children to be buried. I think he was quite shocked by everything that happened, but he mentioned that he'd be interested in helping us write up a report about it all."

"Do you think he's on our side?"

"I think he's trustworthy," she replied, "and frankly, we could use all the help we can get. I'm not certain, but I'll keep him in the loop. You never know, it might be useful one day to have a man of the cloth to help us navigate some of the more... unusual aspects of our research."

"You're not getting all religious on me, are you?" he asked disdainfully.

"I'm just keeping an open mind," she told him. "You said it yourself, sometimes that's the most important thing."

"Speaking of which," he added as he took the soup off the hob and set it aside to cool, "I need to do some more tests with Rose this afternoon. I'm still not entirely convinced that she was possessed by that priest, at least not in the conventional sense, but it's quite clear that there's something unusual going on with her. She seems to pick up on the supernatural in a way that the rest of us don't. Alicia's a lot more normal in that regard."

"Do you really think your tests with the cards are going to achieve anything?"

"It's all I've got for now," he said as he kissed her on the cheek and headed to the door. "I'll keep modifying my methods as and when I come up with anything new, though. As you said, there's a lot we don't understand. Hopefully that'll change soon."

Stopping, he glanced back at her.

"By the way, how did it go with your mum? Did you persuade her to get some kind of stair system installed so that she won't fall quite so often."

"Not a chance," she admitted wearily. "You know what Mum's like. She can be so stubborn sometimes."

"Oh, believe me, I'm fully aware of that fact," he replied with a faint smile. "I'm pretty sure that's where you and Alicia have got *your* stubbornness from as well."

"I'm not sure that it's stubbornness in this case," Rebecca told him. "I think she just... genuinely believes that she can hold back time. That she doesn't ever have to get old."

***

"The four of... spades," Rose said several hours later, furrowing her brow as she looked at the decorated side of the playing card Jonathan was holding up. "Or diamonds. No, spades."

"Are you sure?" he asked.

She nodded.

"Are you *really* sure?"

She nodded again.

"Okay, Rose," he continued, still holding the card up, "I'm going to ask you one more time to really think hard and -"

"I'm sure," she said firmly, unable to hide a sense of irritation. "Why do you keep asking me about the same card?"

"Because I want to be certain that you're really trying," he said, glancing at the queen of hearts he was still holding. "It's important that you don't just say the first thing that comes into your head."

"I don't know what you want me to do," she continued. "I've tried to see what the card is, it's not my fault if I can't do it."

"If -"

"This is so stupid," she added, interrupting him again. "How many times are you going to keep doing these tests before you admit that they're never going to work? I can't see through a piece of card! I want to stop."

"We just have a few more to do today."

"How many?"

"Not *that* many."

"I want to know," she replied, before pulling the wires away and climbing off the chair. "I'm bored. I don't want to do this. I've tried enough times and it obviously isn't going to work."

"Rose, please sit back down," Jonathan said as she headed to the door. "Please, I just need to refine the methodology a little bit and then I'll try to find a way to make it more fun. I promise."

"I don't want to!" she said firmly as she hurried away and disappeared from view. "Why won't you just leave me alone? I'm not some kind of freak!"

"No-one's calling you a freak!" he called after her, but she was already gone.

He sighed.

"Not to your face," he muttered under his breath.

Leaning back, he looked at the card and set it down, and then he looked at all the other cards in the pile. Grabbing his notebook, he began to flick through the various pages and he saw the columns of crosses everywhere, with some of the data having been gathered more than a week earlier. For a few minutes he was lost in thought, trying to come up with some other way to analyze Rose's apparent abilities, until finally he heard footsteps and he turned to see that Rebecca was making her way through.

"Are you done already?" she asked.

"We are."

"I thought -"

"Rose decided to call it a day early," he added. "She clearly wasn't in the right mood. We ran through hundreds and hundreds of cards but she was getting more and more ratty with each one."

"She's still just a kid," she pointed out. "She's only ten years old, even if sometimes she seems so very mature. I'm sure she'll come around eventually."

Staring at the notebooks, Jonathan began to notice something a little odd. He flicked through to some of the earlier sessions and began to mutter to himself as he tried to make a few calculations in his head.

"What is it?" Rebecca asked. "I've seen you like this before, Jonathan. It usually means that you've got an idea."

"The odds of guessing the right card – and I mean purely guessing, with no powers or anything special – are obviously one in fifty-two each time."

"Sure, but -"

"Which means that the odds of guessing

wrong are fifty-one in fifty-two, or about ninety-eight per cent. Give or take."

"I know how probability works. What are you -"

"If I asked Rose to simply guess the card, she should therefore get it right purely randomly about one in every fifty-something tries. Obviously the number will be a little different in real life, but in all the sessions before today that was basically what was happening. She wasn't doing any better than she would have if she'd been guessing randomly, which to be honest might have been what she was doing the whole time."

"And it was the same today?"

"No," he said with a growing hint of wonder in his voice as he continued to flick through the notes. "No, today was different."

"She got better at guessing?"

"She was angry at me," he continued. "Right from the start, I could tell that she really wasn't in the mood to be doing this at all. She was complaining about it and saying it was pointless, and her anger was directed *at* me."

"Don't take it personally."

"I'm not, but don't you get it? She was so annoyed at me for making her do these tests. For the first time, she was actively pissed off at me." He held the notebook up so that she could see the columns, and then he began to turn from one page to the next. "Don't you see what happened?"

"She didn't do very well."

"She got every single card wrong," he pointed out firmly. "Out of more than a thousand. Statistically speaking, that's as significant as getting lots right. If she was just guessing, she still should have got a few of them correct. The odds of getting none out of a thousand are extremely low." He looked one of the pages. "But because she was angry," he added, "she was able to get them *all* wrong out of spite. It's not what I expected to happen, but in a way this still proves my point."

He stared at the page for a moment longer before turning to his wife, and he immediately saw that she understood the point he was trying to get across.

"She *does* have some kind of power," he added turning to another page, revealing nothing but column after column after column of crosses. "This experiment just proved it beyond doubt."

EPILOGUE

Eight years later...

"ALRIGHT, ALRIGHT!" A VOICE called out in the darkness. "Keep your hair on! I'm awake, just... you'll have to give me a moment!"

A light flickered on somewhere upstairs, and a few seconds later the voice let out a sigh. Something heavy briefly rattled, followed by a sudden whirring sound as the stair lift began to slowly descend. Finally Evelyn Ward appeared, frail and dressed in her nightgown with her white hair looking particularly unkempt as it hung down on either side of her face. The stair lift itself appeared to be in no hurry as it carefully maneuvered its way around a slight bend in the stairs, and Evelyn could be heard letting out a series of impatient tuts and sighs as she waited to reach the hallway.

Already, someone was banging on the front door again.

"Alright!" Evelyn snapped angrily. "It's gone midnight! This had... it had better be important."

She waited a few more seconds before the stair lift finally locked into position at the bottom, and then she painfully hauled herself up. Her swollen, arthritic hands gripped the handles and her knees clicked loudly as she shuffled toward the door, and then she hesitated as she reached up to slide the chain out of the way. Part of her was hoping that the strange knocking sound had just been some kind of prank, and that she was going to be left alone, although deep down she knew that the disturbance had been far too insistent, almost as if -

"Evelyn!" a familiar voice called out suddenly as the knocking returned. "Evelyn, it's me!"

"What the..."

Startled, Evelyn furrowed her brow for a few seconds before fumbling with the chain, which finally came loose after a few more attempts. Reaching down, she turned the key in the lock and finally she pulled the door open. Staring out onto the porch with an expression of horror, she wasn't quite sure whether she could believe what she was seeing with her own two eyes.

"It's the small hours!" she gasped. "What... what are you doing here so late?"

She waited, but in that moment she realized that something must be terribly wrong. She opened her mouth to ask what had happened, yet on some level she instinctively understood. After all, Rose had never turned up unexpectedly in the middle of the night before, and she'd never banged on the door like a maniac, and she'd certainly never arrived with so many tears in her eyes.

"What is it?" Evelyn asked, trying not to panic. "Rose, what's happening?"

"It's... it's the others," Rose sobbed as tears ran down her face. "It's Rebecca and Jonathan, and Father Rashford too. We went to Quist House, they made me wait outside in the van like an idiot, I knew I should never have listened to them but Rebecca said she had a plan! She swore she knew what she was doing and that she'd thought of everything and I'm such an idiot because I believed her!"

"What are you talking about?" Evelyn replied, before looking her up and down for a moment. "That's Alicia's jacket, isn't it? The one I gave to her? It used to belong to my husband."

She waited for Rose to answer, but in truth she knew she was only delaying the inevitable.

"Rose," she continued, reaching out and touching the side of the girl's arm. "What's happening, Rose?" she asked. "Did... did something happen on one of those infernal investigations? Rose, talk to me."

Again she waited.

Again she felt the pain and fear in her chest.

Just like last time.

"We lost Alicia," she said softly. "Please, I can't lose anyone else."

"Quist House!" Rose stammered, almost tripping over the words in her frantic desperation to get them out. "The thing, the thing in Quist House. It killed them all. I saved the girl but it got everyone else. Evelyn, I couldn't save them. I tried but I was too late."

"You're... you're not making any sense," Evelyn replied. "Rose... where's Jonathan? Where's Father Rashford? Where... where's Rebecca?"

She grabbed her by the shoulders.

"Where's my daughter?"

"They're dead," Rose sobbed. "All of them. I'm so sorry, Evelyn. Rebecca and the others are all dead!"

Coming soon

**The Haunting of the King's Head
(The Ghosts of Rose Radcliffe book 5)**

Having encountered numerous ghosts now, Rebecca and Jonathan Pearson finally set out to tackle a case together. And when they learn of the supposed haunting of a nearby pub, they think they've found the perfect location. They have no idea that they're about to experience their most terrifying case yet.

For hundreds of years, The Saracen's Head has been a quiet back-street pub in a quiet little English town. Rumors persist, however, that some of the old regulars have never quite left the building. A young boy is sometimes seen standing at the front door, and a ghostly woman dressed all in black has occasionally been spotted in the rooms upstairs. As far as the current landlord is concerned, the dead have unfinished business.

As they get to work, however, Rebecca and Jonathan soon discover that they have very different ideas about how to proceed – and about the causes of the haunting in the first place. Before long, however, they realize that this particular case has its roots in a tragedy that happened many years ago, and that the effects of this tragedy are still

AMY CROSS

Books in this series

More coming soon

Also by Amy Cross

1689
(The Haunting of Hadlow House book 1)

All Richard Hadlow wants is a happy family and a peaceful home. Having built the perfect house deep in the Kent countryside, now all he needs is a wife. He's about to discover, however, that even the most perfectly-laid plans can go horribly and tragically wrong.

The year is 1689 and England is in the grip of turmoil. A pretender is trying to take the throne, but Richard has no interest in the affairs of his country. He only cares about finding the perfect wife and giving her a perfect life. But someone – or something – at his newly-built house has other ideas. Is Richard's new life about to be destroyed forever?

Hadlow House is brand new, but already there are strange whispers in the corridors and unexplained noises at night. Has Richard been unlucky, is his new wife simply imagining things, or is a dark secret from the past about to rise up and deliver Richard's worst nightmare?
Who wins when the past and the present collide?

Also by Amy Cross

If You Didn't Like Me Then, You Probably Won't Like Me Now

One year ago, Sheryl and her friends did something bad. Really bad. They ritually humiliated local girl Rachel Ritter, before posting the video online for all to see. After that night, Rachel left town and was never seen again. Until now.

Late one night, Sheryl and her friends realize that Rachel's back. At first they think there's on reason to be concerned, but a series of strange events soon convince them that they need to be worried. On the outside, Rachel acts as if all is forgiven, but she's hiding a shocking secret that soon starts to have deadly consequences.

By the time they understand the full horror of Rachel's plans, Sheryl and her friends might be too late to save themselves. Is Rachel really out for revenge? What does she have in store for her tormentors? And just how far is she willing to go? Would she, for example, do something that nobody in all of human history has ever managed to achieve?

If You Didn't Like Me Then, You Probably Won't Like Me Now is a horror novel about the surprising nature of revenge, about the power of hatred, and about the future of humanity.

Also by Amy Cross

The Soul Auction

"I saw a woman on the beach. I watched her face a demon."

Thirty years after her mother's death, Alice Ashcroft is drawn back to the coastal English town of Curridge. Somebody in Curridge has been reviewing Alice's novels online, and in those reviews there have been tantalizing hints at a hidden truth. A truth that seems to be linked to her dead mother.

"Thirty years ago, there was a soul auction."

Once she reaches Curridge, Alice finds strange things happening all around her. Something attacks her car. A figure watches her on the beach at night. And when she tries to find the person who has been reviewing her books, she makes a horrific discovery.

What really happened to Alice's mother thirty years ago? Who was she talking to, just moments before dropping dead on the beach? What caused a huge rockfall that nearly tore a nearby cliff-face in half? And what sinister presence is lurking in the grounds of the local church?

Also by Amy Cross

American Coven

He kidnapped three women and held them in his basement. He thought they couldn't fight back. He was wrong...

Snatched from the street near her home, Holly Carter is taken to a rural house and thrown down into a stone basement. She meets two other women who have also been kidnapped, and soon Holly learns about the horrific rituals that take place in the house. Eventually, she's called upstairs to take her place in the ice bath.

As her nightmare continues, however, Holly learns about a mysterious power that exists in the basement, and which the three women might be able to harness. When they finally manage to get through the metal door, however, the women have no idea that their fight for freedom is going to stretch out for more than a decade, or that it will culminate in a final, devastating demonstration of their new-found powers.

AMY CROSS

Also by Amy Cross

The Ash House

Why would anyone ever return to a haunted house?

For Diane Mercer the answer is simple. She's dying of cancer, and she wants to know once and for all whether ghosts are real.

Heading home with her young son, Diane is determined to find out whether the stories are real. After all, everyone else claimed to see and hear strange things in the house over the years. Everyone except Diane had some kind of experience in the house, or in the little ash house in the yard.

As Diane explores the house where she grew up, however, her son is exploring the yard and the forest. And while his mother might be struggling to come to terms with her own impending death, Daniel Mercer is puzzled by fleeting appearances of a strange little girl who seems drawn to the ash house, and by strange, rasping coughs that he keeps hearing at night.

The Ash House is a horror novel about a woman who desperately wants to know what will happen to her when she dies, and about a boy who uncovers the shocking truth about a young girl's murder.

Also by Amy Cross

Haunted

Twenty years ago, the ghost of a dead little girl drove Sheriff Michael Blaine to his death.

Now, that same ghost is coming for his daughter.

Returning to the small town where she grew up, Alex Roberts is determined to live a normal, quiet life. For the residents of Railham, however, she's an unwelcome reminder of the town's darkest hour.

Twenty years ago, nine-year-old Mo Garvey was found brutally murdered in a nearby forest. Everyone thinks that Alex's father was responsible, but if the killer was brought to justice, why is the ghost of Mo Garvey still after revenge?

And how far will the real killer go to protect his secret, when Alex starts getting closer to the truth?

Haunted is a horror novel about a woman who has to face her past, about a town that would rather forget, and about a little girl who refuses to let death stand in her way.

AMY CROSS

AMY CROSS

AMY CROSS

Also by Amy Cross

The Haunting of Saward Island

Trying to fix their damaged boat, Jacqui Sinclair and her family stop at a remote island that doesn't appear on any maps. They soon discover the horrifying secret that caused previous generations to hide the island's existence from the rest of the world.

Many years ago, the island was the scene of an unspeakable tragedy. Ever since, a malevolent spirit has been lurking in the long grass, waiting near a bare wooden cross for its chance to gain revenge. For Jacqui and the others, their only hope lies in deciphering the clues left behind at a remote lighthouse, where a skeleton crew once tried and failed to defeat the same evil force.

If they fail, the Sinclairs will meet the same grisly fate that has befallen all those who have made the fatal mistake of setting foot on Saward Island...

AMY CROSS

Also by Amy Cross

13 Nights in Crowford

A murdered woman lingers in the old school, waiting for someone to uncover the identity of her killer. A dying painter arrives in the town and finds himself drawn into a nun's final mission. A hunted man takes refuge in an old seaside hotel but finds more than he bargained for. A man returns home after the war, but what dark secret is he hiding?

On the southern coast of England, the town of Crowford has long had a reputation for ghosts. Some even say that the town is home to more ghosts than people. Almost every part of Crowford is haunted, and to prove that claim, here are thirteen stories about the town's mysterious past – from the days before the town had even been founded, through the years of the English Civil War and the era of the Victorians, and on to the horrors and terrors of the twentieth and twenty-first centuries. Together these stories tell the tales not only of Crowford's inhabitants but also of the town itself.

This omnibus edition collects together, for the first time, 13 standalone titles from the Ghosts of Crowford series

AMY CROSS

BOOKS BY AMY CROSS

1. Dark Season: The Complete First Series (2011)
2. Werewolves of Soho (Lupine Howl book 1) (2012)
3. Werewolves of the Other London (Lupine Howl book 2) (2012)
4. Ghosts: The Complete Series (2012)
5. Dark Season: The Complete Second Series (2012)
6. The Children of Black Annis (Lupine Howl book 3) (2012)
7. Destiny of the Last Wolf (Lupine Howl book 4) (2012)
8. Asylum (The Asylum Trilogy book 1) (2012)
9. Dark Season: The Complete Third Series (2013)
10. Devil's Briar (2013)
11. Broken Blue (The Broken Trilogy book 1) (2013)
12. The Night Girl (2013)
13. Days 1 to 4 (Mass Extinction Event book 1) (2013)
14. Days 5 to 8 (Mass Extinction Event book 2) (2013)
15. The Library (The Library Chronicles book 1) (2013)
16. American Coven (2013)
17. Werewolves of Sangreth (Lupine Howl book 5) (2013)
18. Broken White (The Broken Trilogy book 2) (2013)
19. Grave Girl (Grave Girl book 1) (2013)
20. Other People's Bodies (2013)
21. The Shades (2013)
22. The Vampire's Grave and Other Stories (2013)
23. Darper Danver: The Complete First Series (2013)
24. The Hollow Church (2013)
25. The Dead and the Dying (2013)
26. Days 9 to 16 (Mass Extinction Event book 3) (2013)
27. The Girl Who Never Came Back (2013)
28. Ward Z (The Ward Z Series book 1) (2013)
29. Journey to the Library (The Library Chronicles book 2) (2014)
30. The Vampires of Tor Cliff Asylum (2014)
31. The Family Man (2014)
32. The Devil's Blade (2014)
33. The Immortal Wolf (Lupine Howl book 6) (2014)
34. The Dying Streets (Detective Laura Foster book 1) (2014)
35. The Stars My Home (2014)
36. The Ghost in the Rain and Other Stories (2014)
37. Ghosts of the River Thames (The Robinson Chronicles book 1) (2014)
38. The Wolves of Cur'eath (2014)
39. Days 46 to 53 (Mass Extinction Event book 4) (2014)
40. The Man Who Saw the Face of the World (2014)
41. The Art of Dying (Detective Laura Foster book 2) (2014)
42. Raven Revivals (Grave Girl book 2) (2014)

AMY CROSS

AMY CROSS

For more information, visit:

www.amycross.com

AMY CROSS

Printed in Great Britain
by Amazon